RAZORBILL

black HEART blue

black HEART blue

LOUISA REID

razOr bill

PENGUIN

RAZORBILL

Published by the Penguin Group
Penguin Books Ltd, 80 Strand, London WC2R ORL, England
Penguin Group (USA) Inc., 375 Hudson Street, New York, New York 10014, USA
Penguin Group (Canada), 90 Eglinton Avenue East, Suite 700, Toronto, Ontario, Canada M4P 2P3
(a division of Pearson Penguin Canada Inc.)
Penguin Ireland, 25 St Stephen's Green, Dublin 2, Ireland (a division of Penguin Books Ltd)
Penguin Group (Australia), 250 Camberwell Road, Camberwell, Victoria 3124, Australia
(a division of Pearson Australia Group Pty Ltd)
Penguin Books India Pvt Ltd, 11 Community Centre, Panchsheel Park, New Delhi – 110 017, India
Penguin Group (NZ), 67 Apollo Drive, Rosedale, Auckland 0632, New Zealand
(a division of Pearson New Zealand Ltd)
Penguin Books (South Africa) (Pty) Ltd, Block D, Rosebank Office Park, 181 Jan Smuts Avenue,
Parktown North, Gauteng 2193, South Africa

Penguin Books Ltd, Registered Offices: 80 Strand, London WC2R ORL, England

penguin.com

First published in Razorbill, an imprint of Penguin Books Ltd, 2012
001 – 10 9 8 7 6 5 4 3 2 1

Text copyright © Louisa Reid, 2012
'Daddy' taken from *Ariel* copyright © the Estate of Sylvia Plath
and reprinted by permission of Faber and Faber Ltd
All rights reserved

The moral right of the author has been asserted

Set in Garamond MT Std 12.5/14.75
Typeset by Palimpsest Book Production Limited, Falkirk, Stirlingshire
Printed in Great Britain by Clays Ltd, St Ives plc

British Library Cataloguing in Publication Data
A CIP catalogue record for this book is available from the British Library

ISBN: 978–0–141–34270–2

www.greenpenguin.co.uk

ALWAYS LEARNING   **PEARSON**

For anyone who's ever felt different.
And Alistair, Eve and Scarlett. Of course.

You do not do, you do not do
Any more, black shoe
In which I have lived like a foot
For thirty years, poor and white,
Barely daring to breathe or Achoo.

'Daddy', Sylvia Plath

PART ONE
Rebecca and Hephzi

Rebecca

After

They tried to make me go to my sister's funeral today. In the end I had to give in. The black dress Hephzibah had worn last year when Granny died hung heavy from my bones and I wore it like armour. She'd always been bigger. Born first, stronger, prettier, the popular twin. I'd been walking in her shadow for sixteen years and I liked its cool darkness; it was a safe place to hide. Now I shivered in the stark January air. It was the first day of the New Year and my sister had been dead for one whole week.

Granny had been kind and we'd looked forward to staying with her like other kids look forward to Christmas. It was a chance to eat chocolate and watch television. A chance to read books until well past bedtime. At Granny's we were allowed to laugh out loud and play dress up, she even let us try her make-up. Hephzi loved make-up, the more sparkly the better. Granny made sure my sister got a bra when she was twelve and started to show. Sometimes she'd take us to the cinema and we would watch unsuitable films: Disney princesses, cartoons, Harry Potter. She was The Mother's mother and she loved us. She used to kiss me and tell me I was lovely. Her little love. No one else ever said that. As we got older we visited her less and less. No need, said The Parents, we could make ourselves useful at their church events instead of lounging about at Granny's. Years yawned wide with her absence. I know Granny missed us. When she rang up and one of us managed to answer, her voice sounded thin and far away like a paper aeroplane spiralling out of sight. And then she died.

I've recorded today as another black day and it's there, a story inscribed hard on my heart. The tales I keep hidden within are many; if you ever open me up then you'll read the truth. Look inside, peel back skin and flesh, excavate bone, and there you'll find a library of pain. Perhaps you will ask me to explain. I am, after all, the curator of this past. But some things are too terrible to tell and those words are buried deep. Those are the words I never even whispered to my sister, those are the words that I daren't say aloud. I wish they wouldn't cry in the walls of my room and hunt me down in my dreams.

There's a scar on my heart for when Granny died and one for the day Hephzi first didn't want to walk home with me from school. I had to lie to explain away her absence when I arrived back at the vicarage alone; I said she was doing extra maths. This was when we started college in September, four months ago. At college everyone noticed how pretty and sweet and funny my twin was and soon she was being invited to parties and talking to boys.

Because I was her sister I didn't get picked on all that much but I think the other kids laughed at me behind my back. Maybe Hephzibah did too. No one would meet my eyes. Even the teachers found it hard.

But now she's dead. And it was her funeral today. The coffin was white. The Mother cried. The Father presided over the ceremony. When the good God-bothering folk of the village asked him how he could bear it, he said he had to, that it was his duty to his daughter. And I stood at the front in Hephzi's black dress and wondered if she could hear what was going on from inside that wooden box and whether she was lonely and cold too. She would know now, for the first time, what it meant to be really left out. Her school friends clustered at the back of the church crying. He couldn't forbid them from coming but his frozen gaze made it clear that they weren't welcome. I stared at the floor and loathed them all. Hypocrites. They didn't help us while she was alive, why were they here now when it was far too late? When the service was over no one spoke to me and I was left standing on my own, waiting for The Parents to finish being consoled.

Alone felt wrong; anyone could see me now that Hephzi was gone. There is usually a pair of eyes somewhere, flicking over me in fascination and dread. I feel those looks like they're ants, crawling under my skin. Eventually Auntie Melissa, The Mother's sister, came over and asked me how I was. They'd come all the way from Scotland and I barely recognized her at first, but she ventured an arm around my shoulders and tried to hold me. When I didn't answer her concerned murmurs and shrank away from her touch she backed off. I didn't talk to my aunt because I knew he had his eye on me and I was busy telling Hephzi what they were all doing and listening carefully, hoping that she might answer back.

A week without her has been too long.

But now it's dark and the day is almost over. I'm supposed to sleep in this room still, with the other empty bed just a few feet away. Hephzi's bed. Sometimes I wake up in the middle of the night, disturbed by my own screams and the racket coming from the wall, and for a moment I can see the slight hump of her body there, turned away from me, like always, breathing softly.

Hephzi

Before

OK. So my family are mental. Totally weird. I'm getting out of here one day, no question about it, even if it means I have to leave my sis behind.

The day we start college is the beginning for me. I smell it in the September air of the school, hear it in the bang of the lockers, the shouts and laughter of unfamiliar voices, taste it on my lips when I smile and strangers smile right back. I know I can get free now. I told my mother if she didn't let me go then I'd make her life hell and she must have believed me or somehow persuaded my father. I'm bigger and stronger than her now and I know how to push her around, so I can get my own way sometimes, if I'm lucky. Anyway, we've made it out and it's like someone just gave me the keys to the kingdom. The corridors throng with kids our age, all sorts, different shapes and sizes. I can't wait to talk to them and I can already feel the admiring glances of the boys. That's what interests me most. Boys. I've never had a boyfriend but I'll be getting one super quick, I don't think it will be all that hard. Obviously I'll have to ditch Rebecca first. I can't have her hanging round my neck, weighing me down with her donkey eyes.

You've no idea what it's like having a freak for a sister. I mean, I'm used to it. To me her face is as familiar as my own. But when other people see her for the first time, well, you can't blame them for wanting to throw up. And it's not like she makes it any easier for herself, she won't even try to just chat about normal stuff. I know that we don't do normal in our house but I tell her to at least have a go. If you listen then you can soon pick it up. Mostly I tell her not to be so wet, to get a life, but she's hung up on the whole thing. She just needs to be a bit more like me and quit shivering in my shadow.

By lunchtime I've had enough of her spoiling every- thing and it's a relief to follow everyone else down to the canteen without her. In the queue I start chatting to Daisy and Samara, who I recognize from our tutor group. I'm so excited that it's only when I get to the till that I realize that the lunch isn't actually free and that I'm holding up the line as I pretend to fumble for money in my pocket. Samara, who's just behind me, offers to lend me the one pound fifty and I have to say yes. I hope she'll forget to ask me to pay her back. When we all sit down to eat at a round plastic table they ask me what's wrong with Rebecca. I knew they'd all been whispering. I think quickly about what to say. I don't see why Rebecca has to be so embarrassing all the time. Why should I have to be the one who has to explain everything? I don't say that though. I say she's just got a funny face. End of story.

'Did she have an accident?' asks Samara.

'No. Nothing like that. It's a syndrome, it makes her look a bit weird, that's all.'

'Oh.' Samara and Daisy meet each other's eyes and so I don't explain. I don't tell them the stuff Granny told me and Reb when we were little, that it's something that goes wrong with the way the bones in your face get formed when you're growing inside your mum.

'It's OK though.' I don't think they're convinced that she's normal really (well, ish) and I can see Daisy kicking Samara under the table. But then we talk about other stuff and they invite me to go with them to the pub on Friday so I guess it's OK. They go every week. Apparently you can get in under age really easily if you have fake ID. I tell them I don't, so they promise to sort it. Craig, the tall boy with dark hair who looks good but doesn't say much, knows someone who'll do it for a fiver. A fiver's a lot but I could try to get it from Mother's purse. I wouldn't usually dare but I'm going to have to take some risks if I'm going to get a life. And if she notices then I won't take the blame.

I forget to save some lunch for Rebecca but she doesn't say anything so I don't mention it either and after school I go with Samara to Daisy's house so Reb has to walk home on her own. First I make her promise to cover for me.

It's great to go to a normal house. We knew they existed, Granny had shown us that, but I'd forgotten what it was like not to creep around on tiptoe, not to have to make yourself as small and silent as possible. Daisy's parents are both at work and we go up to her room. She has her own TV, even her own bathroom, and everything is yellow and white – the curtains, the bed-clothes, everything matches. For a minute I just stare. I want to touch each thing: cuddle the soft toys she's got lined up on a shelf, try on her shoes, jump on the big four-poster bed. Daisy puts on music and we go on Face-book. I can't believe she has her own computer up here too. They set up an account for me – it's a bit embarrass-ing to admit I haven't got one already, but they don't say anything and I watch carefully as they use the computer, trying to learn fast. Daisy takes a picture of me on her mobile phone and then uploads it on to my profile. I add them both and now it's just a question of waiting for the friend requests. They do my nails and pluck my eyebrows, laughing when I squeal, and tell me I'm pretty. I haven't had this much fun in my entire life.

It's only when Daisy asks me what it's like having a vicar for a dad that I get a bit uncomfortable.

'Oh. I dunno. Normal, I suppose.'

'Really? Do you have to, like, pray all the time? Go to church every day?'

'It's a bit like that. But sometimes we don't go.' I don't tell them we hide under our beds and play the invisible game. Thank God Samara changes the subject.

'Craig fancies you.'

My insides explode. He's definitely the coolest boy in the year. And he's good looking. Really.

'How do you know?' I try not to look bothered but I can feel I'm blushing. I'll have to get a handle on that.

'He said you were cute.'

Hmm. I'm not sure if that's good enough. What exactly does cute mean? Cute like a puppy or a kitten?

Daisy looks annoyed. 'He never has a girlfriend anyway, so, you know, don't get your hopes up.'

'Oh, OK.'

She changes the subject. 'What was it like being home-schooled anyway? Isn't that really weird?'

'Yeah, it got a bit dull. Just me and Rebecca and Mum.'

'I thought you met up with all the other home-school people? That's what my cousin did. She had loads of mates.'

'Oh yeah, we did that. Course.' There will have to be a lot of lies told, I realize, and I'll have to be careful what I say.

'So what do you think of college, then?'

'It's good. Yeah, I think I'll like it. Everyone's really nice.'

'Yeah, the teachers are OK. Your sister looked a bit gutted though when you left her on her own. She could have come along.'

'No, I don't think so, she wouldn't want to.' No way am I going to have Rebecca cramping my style. Being a twin is boring and Rebecca is extra dull.

'So, are you gonna come to the pub on Friday, then?'

'Maybe, I'll see.'

'You should. Craig'll be there,' Samara says.

I definitely have to go. It's just a question of getting out.

When I eventually get home Rebecca has covered for me so I ignore my parents' suspicious glances and act like I've done nothing wrong. I'd scraped all the nail varnish off as I walked home, leaving a flaky little trail behind me, like that horrible story Granny read to us a couple of times. It was good when the girl shoved the witch in the oven though, Reb and I liked that bit.

It's a prayer evening tonight and there's no avoiding going. Believe me, I've tried. We sit in the freezing cold church hall and shiver. Roderick, my father, claims there are never enough funds to heat the place properly. I look at the others. They're a tragic bunch; a few old dears and some of his fan club, who've come wearing their stinky breath and greasy hair, their eyes are glazed and faraway as if someone's just walloped them over the head with a frying pan. While I sit and despair and try not to listen to my father I think about a way of escaping on Friday night. I'll need something new to wear and wonder about the charity bags. There might be a fresh pile of stuff to root through. I'll have a look later when everyone's gone to bed. I bet Daisy's mum just takes her out shopping when she wants something new. My mother doesn't do shopping. She doesn't do new, full stop. She's sitting there now with her eyes screwed shut and her head bowed, wearing clothes that look like they were meant for an old lady. It's pretty embarrassing, her being such a mess. At least Rebecca and I make an effort, even if for Rebecca all that means is being clean. Sometimes when they want to punish us they lock the bathroom but usually I find a way. There's no way I'm going round looking like I've dipped my head in a chip pan.

After the prayers, the chanting and the healing, Saint Roderick does his meet and greet bit. The opposite of my mother, he preens like a peacock, and I have to stand beside him, all smiles, while people compliment him on his boring old sermon. Yawn.

He grabs my arm on the walk back to the vicarage. A bit too tight.

'Well, Hephzibah. How did you get on at the college today?'

'Fine, thank you.' I try to squirm away but he's not letting go. I'll have a bruise.

'I hope you won't make a habit of being late home. I wouldn't like to think of you walking the streets in the evening all by yourself.' His voice is stretched taut, like a tripwire.

'It's perfectly safe.' Arguing with him is not a sensible thing to do but sometimes I can't help it. And I can push things, further than Rebecca ever can anyway.

'Next time you're planning on staying late, you let me know. I'll be there to collect you.'

Yeah, in your dreams, I think. But I smile and say thanks instead. With a bit of luck he'll be out of it on Friday and I'll get away with sneaking off.

In bed that night I decide it's time to build bridges with Rebecca. She's barely spoken to me this evening and I know it's because I went off without her. Her hurt, hang-dog look is massively annoying but I'm going to pretend I haven't noticed anything's wrong.

'You should have come with us today, Daisy and Samara are so nice. You'd have had fun.'

She's still silent, her face to her wall, scrunched up in bed. She's so thin you'd barely notice she was there.

'What's up? Didn't you like college, then?'

No answer. I heave a martyred sigh and roll over on to my back, way too excited to sleep. I can't wait to go back again tomorrow and see my new friends and Craig. Before I nod off I remember the fiver I need to find and remind myself to get up extra early and sneak a look in Mother's purse.

Rebecca

After

When I woke this morning, it was still January. Still the day after the funeral. Hephzi was still dead. It was over a week now. My head was like lead on the mattress and my throat felt like I had swallowed barbed wire but I still had to get up and leave for college. The new term was starting and if I didn't go in then I might as well give up completely. We were pretending to be normal and The Parents were watching me all the time, making sure I toed a line that was scored like a groove in glass; if I slipped or stumbled then something would shatter. They've always made us keep up appearances, me and Hephzi. Hephzi was always better at that too. She could smile and flutter her eyelashes and say just what they wanted to hear and people would walk away pleased to have spoken to her. She'd picked up those manners from The Father. But today I had something important to do. Just as I'd been about to go home after the funeral, Daisy, one of Hephzibah's newly acquired friends, had brushed past me and shoved a piece of paper at my chest. I'd read the message, torn the note into tiny pieces in the palm of my hand, then let the wind carry them safely away.

Up until September The Mother taught us at home; her specialist subject was misery and lessons of painful silence and glares masqueraded as basic Maths and English. When the Home-School Inspector came to check up on us, they put on a show of course, but mainly she stuck with what she knew best. But when we turned sixteen Hephzi demanded that we study for our A levels. She'd been begging to go to school for years, her voice growing less meek, less mild, and when she found out about A levels from Mrs Sparks she wouldn't shut up about them. The Father took a lot of persuading, and so did the people at the school, but for once the cards were dealt in our favour. The teachers would make arrangements and help us to catch up. It was an unusual situation but allowances could be made. I was glad. I thought we would breathe fresh air at last, away from the septic trail of The Mother's spite. We'd been dying inside as we trod in her footsteps, marking time. I itched to be free but, well, I wasn't sure about the idea of college. Getting out of the house more would be good but it made me nervous. It wasn't me I was worried about, it was my sister.

The Mother hated to think she was doing us a favour by sending us to the school in the village, where we were to enrol at the sixth-form centre. But it was too late by then, they couldn't back out without stirring up talk. Most of the local kids were staying on there and it would be an opportunity for us to try new things, meet some of the locals, have some fun, that's what Mrs Sparks said to me when we bumped into her on the first day we left the vicarage to walk the mile up the main road to the school. Hephzi was thinking about meeting the ones who didn't come to church, the ones we'd never had a chance to make friends with – and that was most of them. We'd seen them though, buying chips in their lunch breaks, smoking on the swings, hanging arm in arm around the village. Hephzi had stared greedy-eyed and I'd watched her wanting them and wished I could steal the view. Then the thought slid through me, a curl of hope, that I might find a friend there too, someone else besides Hephzi who I could talk to. But it didn't work out like that.

Today Craig was waiting, as the note had said he would be, at the Rec. He was sitting on a swing, leaning back and looking up into cold acres of sky. The air was white, white with cold and white with ice, and I pulled my coat around me as I trod over ground that was as dead and as frozen as The Father's heart. But for Craig, the place was empty. No one would see us. As I walked over to him, fighting the wind which drove slivers of cold into my bones, my body ached and I faltered. I could turn and go back the way I had come. I shouldn't even be here. But Craig had spotted me and was sauntering over. I followed him into the kids' playhouse and scrunched myself, small and tight, into a corner. He lit up a cigarette and I inched even further away. Someone had scrawled filthy words on the child-size table and I stared at them as I waited for him to speak first; I had nothing to say. When he'd smoked half his cigarette he spoke, his voice gruff.

'You gonna tell us what happened, then?'

I didn't answer. Why should I tell him anything? He wasn't my friend.

'Look, all I want to know is, how'd she die?'

Again, I didn't respond. This was all he'd wanted, to interrogate me about my dead sister. What else had I been expecting? She was none of his business now. I shifted, still on my feet and ready to go. I should be at school in Physics. There'd be hell if they reported that I hadn't been there.

'Where're you going?'

'Physics.'

'Just wait, would you?'

From outside the playhouse I stared at him then, as he sat in his beanie hat, smoking the cigarette down to the filter, his long legs somehow concertinaed into the tiny space, and wondered why Hephzi had liked him. I knew I was ill. My head ached and my throat was worse. Inside my old coat I was sweating and shivering too. As I turned away to trudge back to civilization I heard him call me a name but I didn't respond. He was nothing to me.

By the time I reached school I knew I really wasn't right. I slumped down in the corridor opposite the reception desk not caring who saw or stared. The bell had gone for second period and dawdling feet scuffed past me in trainers and dirty boots. I watched them go by and wondered if someone would stop. It was a pair of heels which faltered and then drew to a halt.

'Are you all right down there?'

I looked up through my fringe, it was lank and greasy but I didn't care that I hadn't cleaned myself that morning. Without Hephzi to nag me I could be as smelly as I liked.

'It's Rebecca, isn't it?'

I just about managed to nod.

'Hang on, let me get someone.'

The heels clicked away and returned with another pair of feet, this time shod in sensible lace-ups.

'Come on, love, let's get you up.' Strong hands hauled me upright and I lolled in the caretaker's arms. He manoeuvred me to a plastic chair by the reception hatch and I sat, shivering and waiting to see what would happen next. I'd never caused a drama before. In fact I usually made a point of keeping well out of the limelight. Someone was being summoned, the school nurse it turned out, and she took one look at me before she said, 'Call the parents.'

The Mother came for me. She wasn't allowed to drive the car and so she'd walked and it had taken ages. I'd sat there in reception, not caring who stared, and the nurse had periodically come back to check on me. She'd given me a plastic cup of water and two paracetamol but it hadn't made any difference. After twenty minutes or so Craig had sidled in and sloped past, avoiding looking in my direction like always.

When The Mother arrived the nurse appeared again.

'Rebecca's running a high fever and needs to go straight to bed, Mrs Kinsman. I'd ring for a doctor's appointment if I were you.'

The Mother nodded. She looked annoyed.

'Come on, Rebecca. Let's get you home.'

'She's rather weak, I'm afraid. She'll need some help getting to the car.'

'Car? I didn't bring the car. She can walk. The fresh air will do her the power of good.' I heard my mother laugh, a brittle burst which I knew meant she was determined not to be bossed about by a wretched do-gooder. That was what they called people like the school nurse, or the local GP, or my form tutor. Once or twice when I was small, people had come to the vicarage, social workers or doctors or people interested in what I was, I don't really know. They discussed me, and he explained how shy and slow I was and that they were doing their best with me. I would sit on his knee while they stared, not really there, playing invisible, and he would talk and then they'd smile and go away. The Father had explained that we were never to talk to people like that and that we'd only get in trouble if we did. He said that no one liked lying children and that there were special punishments for them. Never trust a do-gooder, he said. Not to their faces, though, to their faces he was as nice as pie.

'You're at the church at the other end of the village, aren't you? Can you phone someone and ask for a lift?'

'I don't think so. Now, Rebecca. Come along.'

I wobbled to my feet and the walls began to spin. The nurse stepped forward, stopped me from toppling and pressed me back into the chair.

'Mrs Kinsman, I understand this is a difficult time for you. But Rebecca really is unwell. She will not be able to walk the length of the High Street. I'll get Linda to call a taxi for you.'

The receptionist made the call and I was too ill to even be frightened at the consequences which would await me back home when The Father saw us arrive in a cab. The Mother didn't say a word to me on the journey; she didn't need to, her silence iced the air between us. She helped me out of the cab though and paid the driver before hustling me inside, looking over her shoulder.

'Where is he?' I managed to croak.

'Out visiting.'

I nodded and crept upstairs, falling into bed fully dressed.

She didn't bring me a drink or any painkillers, I doubt we had any in the house, and I knew she wouldn't call the doctor. They don't like people coming round unless it's on church business, when they can keep them downstairs in the front room and pass round Granny's posh teapot. Occasionally I staggered to the bathroom and drank from the tap. Three days I lay up there alternately sweating and shivering. At the height of my fever, somewhere in the middle of one of those nights, I saw Hephzi sitting on the end of my bed. She smiled, told me to be brave, then, waving and jolly, sank down into the floor, swallowed up by the carpet. I reached for her, to pull her back, but I was too slow and too weak. Again. I'd been begging Hephzi to come back to me and I screamed silently for her, but she'd gone and I fell back into my sweat-starched sheets, as the wall began to cry.

While I lay up there waiting for something to happen, he came. My eyes snapped open, startled out of a dream, to see The Father there in front of our wardrobe, his arms filled with Hephzi's few things. Still as a statue I let my eyelids droop and willed myself invisible. He buried his head in her clothes, moaned, whimpered, crooned, then carried the bundle from the room, not once glancing my way. I was glad I'd hidden my favourite things, her blue jumper, her silver necklace. A tiny vial of perfume a woman in the chemist had given her as a tester when she'd admired the scent. If he was going to come creeping in here like that then I'd have to be even more careful. Nowhere was safe.

It's hard to hide here. That's why we play the invisible game. But The Parents have their secret amusements too, of course, and for a while I'd been a good specimen for him to practise on. But when my face stayed the same regardless of his ministrations he realized I wasn't an adequate example of his power and that he couldn't work miracles despite his hype. He started leaving me behind with Granny again but I can still remember how his special services frightened me. I didn't like to see the other children cry as he exorcised their devils. I wanted to hide. Like a medieval mountebank he travelled the country, peddling false faith and the elixir of eternal life. In the car on the way home The Mother would count their spoils and he would thump the steering wheel with his fist and shout, *Hallelujah! Praise the Lord!*

His very own demon still comes in my dreams and I scream for release as it bundles me and burgles me and breaks me in two.

In the end someone put a stop to his little sideline but he still offered such services under cover of night. We played invisible then and tried not to hear the screams from downstairs.

Eventually I felt better and needed to eat. It was late morning and, pulling my cardigan tightly round me, I tottered downstairs. Sun filtered weakly through the hall window and made dancing patterns on the carpet and wallpaper. I would have some food and then go to college. Even before Hephzi had died I'd decided that if I had to go and study then I might as well try hard and let my exams be my passport out of the vicarage. I couldn't live with them for the rest of my life and this might be a way to escape. The glares of accusation now made it even more obvious that I had to go.

With no one around I made toast and drank orange juice, pouring it shakily from the value pack I'd hauled home from the local shop. The margarine tasted rancid on the bread that had charred in the toaster but I swallowed it nevertheless, not caring. Food was barely a necessity in this house and never a luxury. I stared at the old Formica units and cracked linoleum. The ancient, grimy stove and greasy walls blankly returned my gaze. Even if I had a friend, bringing them here would be out of the question. Hephzi had tried to make our room nice, she'd smuggled in a pot of paint she'd got from Craig's mum, who'd been doing up her living room, and got halfway through painting one wall pale green. That was in the autumn. She hadn't finished it before she died. I wouldn't be taking up the task; I wouldn't go near that wall unless I had to. As I chewed the toast I wondered where The Parents were. The door had slammed about an hour ago. No one had been up to see me that morning and I knew better than to look for a note. If I hurried I would make period four. Maths. I couldn't afford to fall behind in my least favourite subject and knew there'd already be tons to catch up on.

By lunchtime I was tired and took refuge in the library. It had become the place to which I'd retreat most days and the librarian looked up and smiled as I came in.

'Rebecca! I wondered where you'd got to. Are you all right?' Her warmth wrapped me like a blanket and I nodded and smiled back, the feeling funny on my face. I hoped I looked vaguely normal. Once I'd practised in the mirror in the school loo, trying to find the way to move my mouth to make it look less ghastly, but no matter how I tried, my jumble of teeth crowded the expression and I couldn't disguise the ancient graveyard that hid ashamed behind my lips. I always smile with my mouth closed and speak as little as possible.

I made my way over to the back of the library to pick up where I'd left off, halfway through the Cs. I was determined to read every book on every shelf but it was taking me a long time. I couldn't take the novels home and the only time I could read was in the library during lunch or in an odd free period. But I was determined not to give up. Once I was transported to Wuthering Heights or downtown LA I was happy, my world receded and for forty minutes reality hung suspended somewhere over the school like a black balloon waiting to pop as the bell for registration sounded. Today I was finishing off a Raymond Chandler and all through my illness I'd been wondering about the end, making up alternative versions of the story to keep my mind entertained in its more lucid moments. Hephzi hadn't liked to read as much as I did, but sometimes at night if she couldn't sleep she'd wake me up and ask me to tell her a story and I'd fill her in on *Emma* or *Villette* and we'd both nod off again, content. Hephzi wouldn't have liked this one though. She liked the romances and the happy endings. Murder and mystery weren't her style.

On my way out of the library Mrs Larkin stopped me in my tracks.

'Look, Rebecca.' She was holding out a leaflet. 'I saw this and thought of you straight away! It's a summer school.' Seeing my face, she thrust the thing more firmly towards me. 'Here take it – it's something for you to think about at least.'

I took the glossy-looking pamphlet and stared at the photograph of girls and boys sitting together on a green lawn under a beech tree. Their faces were as bright as their futures and they held books open on their laps. Some were reading and some were laughing. I didn't recognize them. 'Cambridge Summer Schools,' the leaflet read, 'for Gifted and Talented Students.' I thrust it back at her, shaking my head.

'Take it, have a think,' she encouraged and, seeing disappointment crease her face at my refusal, I put the thing in my pocket. I'd bin it later. There was no point dreaming; the leaflet was nothing more than a glass slipper handed to the ugly sister. I would never fit in there even if they'd let me go, which was a fairy tale in itself. Mrs Larkin meant well though so I tried my tight smile again and wandered off to registration. As the teacher called names and handed out notices I pulled the leaflet out of my pocket. I couldn't resist the glossy paper, the smiling, intelligent faces. The courses were all for sixth formers and the one Mrs Larkin had underlined jumped out at me immediately. But I wasn't studying English. I did the subjects he'd chosen, things I'd never understand. The idea of studying Literature for a whole two weeks sent a shudder of fear and excitement running to my heart like a little electric shock. I pushed the leaflet into my locker at the end of registration; I would look again tomorrow.

Life at home without Hephzi was hard. She had been the cement which held the bricks of our family together. If you can call us that. I don't like the word, not for us, saying it is like trying to swallow a stone. The Father sort of loved Hephzi. She could make him laugh at her jokes and indulge her whims, he was proud of her sparkle and prettiness.

I remember going carolling when we were eleven. Someone from the church choir had suggested we raise money for charity by singing our way around the village. Songs weren't usually allowed, not for us, but the choirmaster had insisted.

'Hephzibah has a beautiful voice, Vicar, she could do a little solo.' He'd heard her singing as we polished the altar one Saturday. She'd clamped her hand over her mouth too late, only realizing her mistake when he'd stopped crashing out his chords on the organ and turned to listen. We'd hoped he wouldn't tell, but he did.

Hephzi turned her face to The Father, glowing with the praise and excitement.

'Please, Daddy, I'll do my best, I promise, I won't let you down.'

He had to say yes, he couldn't resist, especially with the choir looking on and Mrs Sparks nodding so enthusiastically at his elbow, and so she was granted the chance. He marched round with us – I trailed behind holding the tin for the money and Hephzi sang like an angel at every door.

'How wonderful! How delightful! What a beautiful voice! Isn't she sweet?' people said and put their spare change in my rattling pot. Despite himself, The Father swelled up and basked in her glory. But it never happened again, even though she begged for another chance. It would lead her to sin, that was his view, and all songs ceased but for the psalms we chanted in church.

Now with Hephzi gone he was more morose than he'd ever been. And bitter. That sharp, acid anger directed itself at me, the one who'd survived. The one who ought to have died.

They blamed me for bringing the spotlight on to the household and making it harder for them to do as they pleased. The Father hated me because the thing he'd liked to watch over, like a greedy vulture, was gone and now they had to be careful, extra vigilant, just in case any more questions were asked. But I blame myself too. I should have saved her. That was my job.

'So you actually got up today, then,' he barked at me when I returned home after college. I'd had to walk the mile home of course, and had struggled through the darkening after-noon, skidding my way over patches of black ice as my shoes soaked up slush. I'd had no lunch and just swallowed a few mouthfuls of water from the fountain by the nurse's office during afternoon break. My knees were trembling. All I wanted was to creep up to bed.

I nodded in reply, knowing better than to look up at him and meet his eyes. Just the sight of me could often enrage him.

'You'd better get to the kitchen and help your mother.' I'd been let off lightly and hurried away. The Mother was emptying canned carrots into a pan. A joint of meat sat in its tin, leathery and dry. She always overcooked things.

'Can I help?'

'Set the table.' She glanced up briefly from her tasks and I noticed how washed out she looked, like one of the dish rags hanging miserably from the taps. Her eyes were the same pale blue as mine, the colour of the early morning winter sky, and I wondered if she'd ever noticed. Hephzi had had big, beguiling brown eyes and long lashes which scudded over her cheeks like fluttering wings. You wouldn't ever have guessed we were twins and I could tell Hephzi had been glad. When it suited she could pretend we'd never even met.

She pinches me when I think things like that. I brush away her fingers and tell her not to deny it; she knows it's true. I would try to make her talk to me later. If she was really here then I wanted her back properly, not just listening in then disappearing again, leaving me all by myself.

We ate in silence. I chewed my food carefully, trying to make it easier to swallow, but I could feel bits of tough meat and gristle lodging themselves in the crooked nooks and crannies of my mouth. They would be impossible to dislodge. It was hard to eat with my mouth closed though, hard to be invisible. Every so often The Father looked up at me in disgust, ready and waiting to pounce. He stared at me, with that fixed gaze, so deep blue it was almost black, and I tried to be more silent, not to clatter my cutlery or slurp my drink, to masticate noiselessly. Eventually I decided to swallow the food whole to avoid the snarl and I could see The Mother do the same, cutting the pieces of meat so small they would slither down her throat. Tonight would be one of his nights, you could feel it in the air.

When he drank Hephzi and I had often been relieved. Sometimes it meant we could disappear out of range, go upstairs and whisper and giggle instead of being forced to remain under his vigilant gaze, reading the pieces of scripture he'd prepared earlier that day and then being quizzed and questioned on the obscure tenets of his faith. I don't believe in his God. He's never come to help me or my sister and that's all the proof I need. And as for love. Well, if God was love then he'd died with my granny. As if The Father somehow knew my treacherous thoughts, he'd fire the hardest questions my way, pushing me and pushing me to say something I would regret. Then Hephzi would start to cry. She hated to watch when he started on me, and sometimes there'd be a reprieve. So when he was busy with his bottle we were usually safe. Usually.

Going to bed early was a good idea. If I'd had a key to my room I'd have locked myself in. The Father kept the key. But at least he never came in. He's always done his dirty business downstairs, as if that makes it OK. I pushed Hephzi's bed against the door and hoped she wouldn't be angry.

'Is that OK, Hephz? I don't want him to come in,' I whispered.

There was no answer. Again.

So instead I imagined she was playing invisible and I joined in and we carried on like that until I went to sleep.

Hephzi

Before

Here's what I think of college so far. Firstly, the work sucks, especially the homework. Thankfully Rebecca is doing mine for me, even though I can tell she hates it too. Secondly, the teachers are boring and have no idea what it's like to be young and want to have fun. They drone on for hours and hours and hours which is basically my idea of torture. Lastly, my new friends are fantastic and I'm having the best time of my life. Hallelujah!

Well, mostly I am.

The thing is you have to be careful what you say round here. When I'm with Reb I can say what I like and she knows mostly everything I think without me having to open my mouth. But here! There's things you have to think, things you have to say. Things you definitely can't say because if you do people will hate you.

You have to think Daisy is the prettiest girl in Year Twelve, and the most popular. You have to think that she'll definitely get the part in the school show they're going to do at Christmas. I wish I could audition, it's a musical, but I know there's no point.

You also have to laugh at the teachers and call them names. That's quite funny, but I didn't expect it.

You have to really not start a row in the common room. I found that out the other day when they were all talking about this boy, Sam, who I'd actually thought was quite sweet. He asks how I am every day and says he likes my outfit, even if I know that he knows that it's the same as yesterday's. Well, I thought maybe he even fancied me, until Samara told me about him.

'Sam's met a new guy, from the sixth-form college in town, I saw them together. He's adorable.'

'Sam who?' I thought she must be talking about someone else, one of their friends who I'd yet to meet.

'You know Sam Roberts? In our tutor group? I met his new boyfriend last Saturday.'

'What? He's a homosexual? Really? That is disgusting!' My voice was loud and the whole place fell silent. I didn't know what I'd said wrong. Someone sniggered on the other side of the common room.

'What? Are you a homophobe or something?' challenged Daisy. I didn't know what that was and looked at Samara, hoping she'd explain.

'D'you hate gays?' she said, darting her eyes at the others.

'Well, they're dirty, aren't they? It's like, you know, totally evil what they do. It's a sin.' I'd heard my father preach about it. I didn't listen mostly but I must have tuned in for that one. I should have known better than to repeat anything I'd heard in the church or at my father's table but the words had come out before I'd had time to remember to keep my big mouth shut. I searched the room for Rebecca to see if she'd heard, looking for her to get me out of trouble, but we were at college and college meant staying apart.

'God! What planet are you from?' sneered Daisy, and she shook her head and gave me the hard look I'd seen her level at others who she thought were odd or stupid or ugly. I laughed then and forced myself to meet her eyes.

'Oh my God! It was a joke!' I cried. 'Of course I don't hate gay people! I was just messing around!'

No one looked convinced and I laid it on even thicker. 'Of course I know Sam's gay, he told me himself. Is his boyfriend really that good looking, then?'

Samara nodded and helped me out by describing him and I oohed and ahhed and breathed a sigh of relief as my cheeks returned to their normal colour. But I bit my tongue for the rest of the day and kept checking no one was whispering about me. I'm being especially nice to Sam too and I've made sure everyone sees me talking to him. But I'm still not certain that Daisy's forgotten what I said and I press it to the back of my mind with a whole stack of other stuff I'm not dealing with right now.

And I do like Sam. I'm not just pretending. He is the opposite of evil. There's another thing Roderick Kinsman got wrong.

From now on I think before I speak. I copy what the

others do and say and I make myself blend in.

Craig bunks off quite a bit. I haven't dared to yet but once I'm his girlfriend I'm going to see what it's like. I haven't escaped from the vicarage just to sit in a classroom all day and be bored to death. Even Rebecca hates it, but then she never wanted to come in the first place. I don't know what she wanted, how else she imagined we'd ever break away from them. She should be thanking me instead of giving me the silent treatment. I've done my best to be nice but she's in a major strop. Well, I've got new friends now, so who cares?

Tonight we're going to the pub. I nicked the fiver from Mother's bag – she hasn't said anything but she must have noticed because it was the only money that was in there. Craig handed me my fake ID today. It's so cool. I'm going round to Daisy's to get ready and she told me I could borrow her new Topshop jeans. We're the same size and I have a black top I can wear with them. I found it at the bottom of one of the charity bags last night and washed it out in the bathroom sink when I was sure everyone was asleep. It should be OK. The logistics of getting out of the house are a bit of a worry but I reckon if I pretend I've got a headache and then just slope off no one will notice. Rebecca won't tell, she'd only be for it too. He always has liked hitting her best.

So tonight's the night. I've really got to find a way to get Craig to take more notice of me. Even though Samara says he definitely fancies me, I think it's hard to tell. He's too cool. My stomach's in knots and I'm not sure whether to giggle or vomit. To be sure she'll help, I have to let Rebecca in on the secret. She says nothing but I can see her little huff of disapproval.

'Cover for me. Promise?'

She nods and I give her a quick hug. I'm always a bit shocked to feel how thin she is. Bits of bone stick out of her shoulders and back, and were I to squeeze tight enough I'm sure I could snap her in two. For a moment I sit down on her bed and make an effort.

'Look. Let's be friends again, Reb. I hate it when you're cross with me.'

She looks up at me through her hair, her eyes are sad blue stars in her long face. Then she sighs a huge sigh.

'OK, Hephz,' she whispers. 'Just be careful. OK?'

I nod, jump up and drag her down with me for supper. I'm so excited I can't eat, not that it tastes good anyway, and it seems almost plausible when I excuse myself with a headache and stomach pains. Father looks at me, I can feel his eyes on my back when I go out of the room. But Rebecca will cover for me, I can trust her with my life.

I run all the way to Daisy's so by the time I get there I'm panting and sweaty. It's not a good look but there's time for me to sort myself out. Daisy laughs when she sees the state of me and I can't explain, I just giggle too. In fact we spend most of the time laughing as we get ready. I tell her how lovely she looks and she smiles and I think she's definitely forgiven me for the Sam thing after all because she straightens my hair and lends me the jeans and a top, so in the end the charity thing doesn't even get worn. The one I've borrowed is sparkly and strappy and definitely makes me look eighteen. I grin into the mirror and Daisy grins back. We've been drinking as we've been getting ready and I feel giddy, like I've been on the merry-go-round that comes to the village green once a year. Our Auntie Melissa took me once, just me for some reason, I can't remember why Rebecca didn't come too. I must have been about four years old and I remember the thrill, the screaming for joy, the way the horses rose higher and higher like they might take off and fly up into the summer evening. But there was a terrible row afterwards and I never went again. Auntie Melissa never comes to see us now.

Daisy has to hold my arm as we totter out of the house on her high heels and down to the bus stop. I try not to feel sick. That would ruin everything. I guess it's not cool to puke up everywhere but, since I've never had alcohol before, I didn't know it would happen like this. I've seen the state of my father when he's been drinking, his red face and eyes, his lurching, swaying body, but when Daisy gave me the fizzy drink it tasted good, sweet and sticky, and I didn't imagine I'd actually feel so wasted so fast.

Daisy tells me to sober up on the bus and I try my best but when we get off at the next village I have to be sick into a hedge. I hope no one from college sees. This is seriously embarrassing. My stomach churns and I heave again but all that comes up is burning liquid and then green bile. I lean against the bus shelter shaking, a film of sweat beading on my forehead and upper lip and Daisy looks at her watch.

'Come on. Everyone else'll be there by now.'

There's a DJ at this pub tonight, apparently he's good. I wouldn't know but Daisy doesn't want to miss a second more so I totter after her, feeling stupid and kind of wanting to go home. I don't tell her that, she's pissed off with me enough as it is. We walk up to the pub, doing our best to look indubitably eighteen. A crowd of smokers is gathered outside and I flick my eyes quickly over them, not wanting to make eye contact but curious. Craig's lounging on one of the tables, sprawled like a resting cat in the late evening sun. My heart booms and skips and there's that merry-go-round feeling again and I'm almost taking off with excitement. Daisy calls out to him in her flirty voice – I've known her two minutes and can already tell when she's playing that part – and he lifts a languid hand in our direction, cigarette dangling from his mouth, eyebrow coolly raised.

I go straight to the loos when we get inside and try to fix my make-up with the little bits I have in my bag. I've nicked a lip gloss from the chemist and found an eyeshadow at the bottom of one of my mother's drawers. I can't imagine her ever wearing make-up, it must be an antique. Women who put make-up on are harlots, that's what Mother says, so maybe it was never even hers. Or maybe she puts it on sometimes, when it's just her and

Roderick. I know he likes things like that, even though he'd never admit it. I've seen his secret pictures. Samara comes to find me in the loo. She lends me some perfume and gives me a hug. Daisy told her what had happened.

'Poor you. I'm always sick.' She laughs. 'Part of the fun. At least you got it over with early.'

She tells me her parents don't know she drinks at all and that's how she's got to keep it or she'll be grounded forever, and I nod, deciding I have a lot more in common with Samara than with the others. Her mum and dad sound pretty strict, not in my parents' league but bad enough.

We buy Cokes and find somewhere to sit. Daisy's talking to Craig but I don't go over. Instead Samara and I perch on stools in a corner and gossip and she whispers to me that Daisy's fancied Craig since Year Ten. My heart sinks at the news. Daisy's easily the prettiest girl in the pub, her lovely long blonde hair falls round her shoulders and she flicks it back as she laughs and flirts. We watch her for a bit in silence and I sigh and stare at my Coke. I'll have to make it last. After the bus fare and the drink there's only sixty pence left in my purse. I've been scraping this money together over the past week, taking a bit here, a bit there, and on Thursday I found a pound coin on the common-room floor. I hope no one saw me pick it up. People are dancing and it's quite dark in the pub and Samara nudges me to get me to look up. Daisy and Craig are on the dance floor. She's giving it her all and it looks like he's enjoying the bump and grind.

'Daisy's a total slag,' Samara confides and I nod. I'm on what my Maths teacher calls a steep learning curve here.

A couple of other kids from the college sit down with us and we laugh and chat for a while but my heart is so not in it. At ten o'clock I say I have to go and wander off to the bus stop. Daisy's disappeared, so has Craig, and Samara only waves bye and then turns back to her other mates, way too busy and having far too much fun to be bothered if I stay or go.

It's cold on the street in the dark and I'm scared. I cry a bit and wait for the bus. When it comes I can't find my ticket and the driver looks as if he's going to chuck me off until his face softens and he lets me on for nothing. Sitting near the front I lean my head against the cold window and feel the hot air blowing on my ankles. Now I have to get home.

Rebecca

After

I decided to fill in the application form for the summer
school. At first it was just to see how it looked. I'd been
unable to stop wondering what it would be like – after all,
when I was lying upstairs on my bed without Hephzi to
talk to or a book to read I had to find something to do.
Except in my imaginings it wasn't me sitting there on that
lawn in the photo, it was Hephzi. I could never be in a
picture like that. Granny said it didn't matter but I know it
does; no one wants to look at a girl like me unless it's to
stare or laugh. My eyes slope. When I eat and sleep it's
hard to breathe. I was born without ears and a face that's
too long. Granny told me ages ago that it's because of a
syndrome called Treacher Collins. I don't think The Parents even bothered to find out what that meant; to them
it was just a reason to hate me. I know it means I'll never
be lovely like Hephz.

She would have fitted in so well, perfect for the leaflet,
her long shiny golden brown hair, her perfect smile and
laughing wide eyes. They'd have wanted her in the photograph for sure. I imagine her getting up after the picture

has been taken, swinging her bag of books over her shoulder and sailing off into the sunshine for a punt on the river and a picnic in the grass, maybe followed by a trip to the theatre and then coffee and ice cream in a smart cafe where she'd discuss the play's dramatic intensity or superb characterization, or something like that. Except that wasn't Hephzi at all. She'd have been looking for the nearest party, giggling about the boy who liked her, and forgetting to do her homework. I lost count of the number of times she copied her answers from me, but I never really minded. I'd do anything for Hephzi. It was hard to understand that she was gone. One minute alive, the next dead. Sometimes before I go to sleep I put on her pyjamas and lie on top of her mattress with its rust-coloured stains to see if her skin might fit. But it never feels right.

'Hephzi, what do you think?' I muttered quietly. Mrs Larkin had the window open and a gust of wind fluttered the pages just as I spoke. I wondered if that could be a sign.

She didn't answer but I filled in my details: name, address, school. It was easy enough. Mrs Larkin caught me at it and nodded approvingly. I didn't bother telling her I was just filling it in for fun, as part of a game I was playing in my head. She would have thought I was mad. I put the form back in my locker, ready for another day. A fragment of the future.

February came. My sister had been gone for over a month. No one else seemed to remember her. Even when

I dared to make the detour round to Craig's, hiding in the shadows of the street, looking for signs of her and seeing if I could summon her up, I found no evidence that anyone else cared about her going. But of course Craig wasn't sad. He'd never loved her. He'd used her and thrown her away. That's what men do to women, even fathers to their daughters. Hephzi should have seen it all coming. If she'd ever opened her eyes, she'd have known how it goes.

At school there were going to be what they called mock examinations. A mockery indeed. When they put the papers down on the desks and I saw the other kids bend their heads and start to scribble, I understood at last what was expected and tried to read the questions. But it was pointless; I was destined to fail all their tests, destined to prove The Father right. The questions were gobbledygook; all that homework I'd done, all those notes I'd taken, it had all been a waste of time. It wasn't that I wasn't trying my best, it's just that the words started to dance in front of my eyes, numbers winked and jiggled and ran in arpeggios across the page. I couldn't do it. Someone noticed and came over and asked if I was OK. I nodded, hiding behind the hair that hung down on both sides of my face and wiped my cheeks on my sleeve. Afterwards the teacher asked me if everything was all right and said the school understood that it was hard for me and that it'd take things into consideration. I nodded again and wandered off. Because there were exams it meant there were no lessons. I could sit in the library all day if I wanted to and no one would ever know.

Instead of worrying about what The Father was going to say when he found out I'd answered not one question on not one paper I immersed myself in *Great Expectations*. I'd graduated to the Ds now and Dickens was wonderful. I wondered if I could smuggle it home; perhaps I could hide it somewhere really safe. Maybe in Hephzi's bed, surely they wouldn't go looking there? Then I could stay up all night and read this amazing book. I was up to the bit where Pip tells Estella how much he loves her and that she would always be a part of him: part of the good and part of the bad. A part of his very existence, no matter what. The words made me cry and my tears splashed on to the page. The girl opposite me reading *Twilight* looked up and stared. Hephzi would have loved it though and I read it over again, learning the page off by heart so I could recite it for her when she came back. The image of the summer school flashed into my head and I thought that if I got to go then I'd maybe have a room in one of those buildings that had been pictured on the leaflet, a room all to myself with no one in the walls, and I'd be able to read whatever I wanted to and find out all the things I longed to know. I walked over to Mrs Larkin.

'The summer school. How will I pay?'

She looked up from her computer in surprise. 'Well. You'll have to talk to your parents, dear. See if they can find a way. Surely they know how you love reading . . . ?' She tailed off, seeing my face.

Then I blurted, 'I couldn't do my exams.'

'No?' Her voice was gentle, her eyes concerned behind the glasses.

'So I don't think I can go, then. Can I?'

'Talk to your teachers, Rebecca. I'm sure something could be sorted out.' She looked a little bit desperate. I suppose she doesn't usually have this kind of thing land on her plate, usually she's just got the overdue books and kids snogging in the Reference section to bug her.

'Sorry.'

'That's all right. Please, do feel you can talk to me any time, Rebecca.'

Someone like Mrs Larkin wasn't going to be able to fix anything, I realized, and one of the cards I'd been using to build my fragile little castle toppled breezily to the floor. I would have to forget about it now. I put the copy of *Great Expectations* down on her desk and felt her eyes follow me, the ghost of her concern trailing behind me, as useless as Miss Havisham's wedding veil.

That weekend it was business as usual. I spent Saturday helping The Mother to clean the church. It was a large old building. Unusual in its design, admiring visitors always said. To me it was a pain in the neck. And arms and shoulders and thighs. I'd scrubbed the cold stone floors and polished the benches so often and so hard that I knew every ridge in the flags, every crack in the pews and every knot in the wood. We worked silently and I sweated, pausing to rest when she wasn't looking. So I was slower than usual and The Mother had to help me get my bits finished on time. She did so unsmilingly, just so I'd know she wasn't doing it for me but to save a row from erupting. Things had to be ready for Evensong or there'd be trouble later.

As I sat through the service I watched The Father, dignified in his cassock, surplice and scarf. Most people thought he was handsome. Even though really they weren't alike people would say that they could see where Hephzi got her looks. The Mother and I usually took that as a signal to shrink further back and leave them to their limelight. That's how it was. Hephzi and him. The bold and the beautiful. But every rose needs its thorn. When we'd been younger, if he'd been in a good mood, he would make jokes and we'd have to laugh.

'We should pin a sign around your neck, Rebecca. A pound a stare. I'd be a millionaire by the end of the day.'

Or he'd jeer, 'What do you want for Christmas, Rebecca? A new face?'

At least it had made me almost immune to the insults of others. I was offensive to him and he'd always made sure I'd known it. And The Mother, the woman who'd given birth to me, never said a word. She and Hephzi were obliged to smirk and titter while I stepped back a few more paces, letting my hair fall around my face, melting into walls, a ghost of a daughter.

On the way out of church a sign caught my eye. I hadn't been the one to put up this new poster so it must have been one of the wardens who'd tacked it there, maybe

Mrs Sparks. The poster advertised a church summer camp for teens, with those same smiling faces on the leaflet I still had hidden at school in my locker but this time jumping to punch the air, their T-shirts spelling out some evangelical *bon mot*. The dates coincided. I thought about it, saw a seed of a plan and let the idea take root. This could be the perfect alibi and it might just work, if only I had the guts to pull the whole thing off. If I could tell them I was going to one place and then end up somewhere else entirely I'd have exactly what I wanted for a change. And for my sister too. All Hephzi had ever wanted was to escape; if I could get us both out of the vicarage and off to the summer school, she'd be free. I could let her go then, cut my heart strings and whistle her down the wind, up and into the clouds where she would soar at last.

You see, I was right. Hephzi hasn't gone, not yet, not entirely. I k,ept on calling for her, I didn't give up, and in the end she started to answer me back. She's whispering in my ear right now and saying that I shouldn't tell anyone about it. She says that everyone'll think I'm mad. But if I need her she comes, even if I can't stop her from being mean sometimes.

I waited until Sunday evening, again the dried-out serving of meat with some flaccid vegetables collected like sedimentary rock in my stomach. He had been drinking steadily: his duties for the weekend over, he would enjoy himself now. The Mother was cleaning the dishes and I was helping. As I wiped the table, the mouldering cloth leaving a stale smell on my hands, I made my opening gambit.

'Mother. Did you see the advertisement in the church? The summer camp? For young people?'

'No.'

I took a deep breath. 'Well, it's at the end of July. I won't be at college then. Could I possibly go, do you think?'

She didn't answer, just scrubbed the meat pan a little more frantically. I'd never asked for anything, not for years, and now she didn't know how to react. Hephzi had been fairly good at wheedling things out of The Mother; as usual she'd succeeded where I'd failed, like when she'd persuaded The Mother to let her go to the fair with Auntie Melissa, or the time when she'd begged for us to go out for our twelfth birthday.

Eventually she spoke. 'You'll have to ask your father.'

'Oh.' I let my disappointment hang in the air, stale and heavy. She twitched away from the sink, gathering up a bag of rubbish to heave into the cold night. I followed her out to the bin. It was so dark she couldn't see me and I forced myself to reach out and touch her sleeve. Instantly she froze.

'Please, Mother. I really want to go. With Hephzi gone, well, I'm lonely . . .'

Not knowing how she would handle this admission, I was glad I couldn't see her face. I wasn't allowed to have feelings, especially about Hephzi, and the darkness between us shrouded our mutual fear. If she admitted I was human, she'd have to help me. The Mother knew she should help me. She'd been the one to find me in the bathroom when I was thirteen, she'd stood over me while I wiped up the blood and the mess and made me swear not to tell. She said that if I told, then people would know how bad I really was. So I buried the truth in my bedroom, I stashed it safe behind the wall, but it cries to me in the night, it cries and wails and asks to be loved. They all do.

'Let me think about it. I'll see.'

That was good enough for me. I scampered upstairs and pulled on my nightclothes, dragging Hephzi's bed into place and barricading myself in for the night. I lay for a long time, not at all tired, trying to work out how I could pull off my plan. The sticking point was the money. Two hundred and fifty pounds. I didn't have that kind of money and nor did anyone else I knew. Unless I could find a fairy godmother, Cinderella would not be going to the ball.

My teachers were fine about the exams. They let me re-sit and I did a bit better and they cobbled together a half decent report for me. But The Father still spun into a rage, fizzing with gleeful indignation. His anger blew like a bomb, for I'd proved he'd been right all along, he said. As far as he was concerned educating a girl like me was a wasted effort and he had only been going along with it for appearance's sake. Now it had been proved that I was a retard, he could pull me out of that school and get me doing something useful. There was plenty of work to do around the vicarage.

'Please. Give me one more chance.'

He stared at me, surprised I'd spoken up in self-defence and that I'd dared to express a desire. Then his lip twisted and his sneer made me drop my eyes again.

'For what? To prove what we all know? You'll never be anything more than a freak, an aberration. But I'll give you five more months and let you show the rest of the world how pathetic you really are. When you fail these exams in the summer then I'll be proved right. And no one will be able to say I didn't give you every chance.'

I held my breath until I'd escaped upstairs then let out a huge sigh of relief. If he'd stopped me going to college, then that would have been the end; I needed to escape, I needed the exams. I guessed The Mother hadn't yet mentioned the summer camp; if she had he'd have been sure to have brought it up then and there and that would have given him another good excuse to ridicule and belittle me. Hephzi's absence hit me again like a fist in the gut. If she'd still been alive I'd have done better in my exams, I would have had her to talk to and to give me hope.

Don't be pathetic! she says. But I told her that it was true.

She'd been moving further and further away from me, I knew that, but I could have pulled her back and made her remember how much she needed me, how much we needed each other. And she did need me. She needed me to help her with her homework, to cover for her, to lie for her, to back her up. And I needed her for all sorts of reasons. It had been the business with Craig that had really come between us and I was glad I never had to speak to him again, even though I still wandered round to stare at his house sometimes. In a way everything was his fault.

They'd met on the first day. I'd been in the form room during lunchtime, not wanting to brave the canteen and all the new staring faces, the suppressed smirks, the looks of outright horror. Hephzi had gone off without me, she'd said she'd bring me something and I waited all lunchtime for her to return, flicking through my Maths textbook, staring out of the window. I hadn't discovered the library yet and I was thinking that two years of this was going to be almost as bad as two more years in the vicarage trying to make myself invisible. I was tired, worn out by nightmares, and I rested my head on the desk. When Hephzi burst back in with a whole crowd I'd been almost asleep and I looked up, expectant, but she met my eyes and then blanked me, turning back to the group, one of whom was Craig.

She didn't hang around with me after that. She always had someone else to sit next to in all of our lessons and she spent every break and lunch hour in Craig's company, disappearing with him, barely showing up at all in the end. I started to hate him. He didn't even know I was alive.

After the debacle with my exams and school report I got my head down and worked hard. I couldn't afford to slip up again and The Father had said he'd be going to the school parents' evening to find out exactly what I was up to. It wasn't until April so I still had time to try to earn some credit. And I still needed to start making money. On the way home from college I scoured the notice board in the local corner shop. It smelled funny in there, stale bread and mice, and the owner sat reading the red tops, his belly resting on the counter. It was where we did most of the household shopping, Hephzi and I, and once or twice he'd given us a lollipop, which we'd jammed in our mouths and crunched to pieces of sticky, sugary rock before we could be spotted. I'd asked Mrs Larkin about working in the library but she'd regretfully shaken her head and told me to check the board in the shop and so that's what I did. There wasn't much to go on though. Someone wanted a cleaner, but for hours when I'd be at college, and someone else was after a builder which cancelled me out again. The guy behind the counter saw me looking.

'You all right, love?'

I nodded. I didn't want to explain myself to him.

'Looking for anything in particular?'

'No. It's all right, thanks.'

'If you need a job I've one going here.' He looked me up and down. 'You're the vicar's girl, aren't you? You're the one with the twin . . . what happened there, then?'

I shrugged and looked at the floor. *Nosy parker*, Hephzi whispers, *tell him to mind his own bloody business*. But I knew he was just saying what everyone else was thinking. Hephzi's death was common knowledge. How it had happened was my family's dirty secret.

'She had an accident.'

'Terrible that.' He paused and I made for the door, not wanting this chat to go any further.

'Well, if you want a job delivering papers after school, then let me know, I've got a space,' he called as I hurried off.

'Thanks.' I didn't dare ask the pay but guessed it couldn't be much. Leaving the shop I felt a little more cheerful though. I was returning to the vicarage with more than I'd set out with that morning: a job offer and *Middlemarch* in my bag. I'd decided to take the risk and smuggle the contraband home. If Hephzi could get away with sneaking out night after night for clandestine meetings with her lover then I could at least risk reading under the covers. And, even if The Father did find the book, I doubted he could find anything in it to complain about. Why he thought books would corrupt us, I don't know. In some of his sermons he preached the evils of reading, especially anything really good. I watched the congregation shift awkwardly in their pews. Some of them didn't agree with what he was saying, but the crazy ones nodded and zealously acted on his words. They were the type who banned Mickey Mouse, the type who threw party invites in the bin, the type who saw something satanic in the carving of a pumpkin. Parents like Hephzi and I had. Crazies who dressed in normal clothes, who smiled and raised money for charity, crazies who got down on their knees to pray, then, once they were safely behind closed doors, peeled off their masks and let the poison erupt.

Granny had got hold of the first few Harry Potter books at the charity shop near where she lived and I'd devoured them, reading all night long under the covers, knowing I couldn't take the book home and unable to countenance leaving without reaching the end. But I'd never betray Granny and I'd never let on what she'd allowed us to do – if The Father knew even half of it he'd dig her up and kill her all over again. I know it was him who did it, even if no one else thinks so – he hated her and she had to pay.

But I learned a lot from Granny and if I ever have children I know how I'll raise them, safe and happy and free. I'll invite their friends over for teas of pizza, chips and homemade cupcakes. We'll have snowball fights in winter and splash in a paddling pool in the back garden in the summer when it's hot. I'll buy them presents and tell them how wonderful they are. We'll have a puppy and go to Disneyland on the holiday of a lifetime. I'll tell them I love them and that they're perfect in my eyes, beautiful and unique. That's what I'll do, if I ever get the chance. My children will never cry themselves to sleep at night or lie quaking in bed afraid of what the darkness holds.

So I took the job. I didn't confess to The Parents but instead told them I was staying late at school for extra Maths coaching. Maths was my weakest point, or maybe it was Physics. Whatever. They didn't like it but so long as I did my chores when I returned and kept out of the way, they let me live the lie. I wore a hat pulled low over my forehead and tramped the streets with my heavy sack of free papers twice every week. The bag weighed a ton and often I felt faint with tiredness and hunger but I persevered. It paid ten pounds a week. I knew I'd only just have enough to pay for the place at the summer school but I'd posted the application form off regardless and was trusting that somehow, some way, something would go right and The Mother would eventually persuade The Father to allow me to go to church camp. I guess I was stupid to believe they'd never catch me at it, stupid to think no one would see me and report back. After all, I'm kind of unforgettable in the looks department.

I'd saved up forty pounds by the time they found out. Thursday night was delivery night and I'd finished my round by half past six. The nights were getting lighter and even though the March wind whipped up the rubbish on the streets and flapped the papers from my hands, the usually interminable task of posting each paper through letter boxes which closed like traps on my fingers hadn't seemed quite as bad as usual. I was looking forward to adding the crisp ten-pound note to my stash, to going to bed with my book and holding my secrets safe. I talked to Hephzi as I made my way round the village, telling her about the course and asking her for ideas about how to get enough money in time. Her advice was to steal it, to creep into our parents' bedroom and empty The Father's wallet while he was asleep or dead drunk. I shouted her down.

'Too risky, Hephzi, what if he caught me? What then?' *How else will you do it, idiot? You've got to get out.*

We argued like that the whole way round and she'd almost convinced me by the time I got back. For her sake this time I walked down to the estate and on to Craig's road on the way home and paused to see if we could spot him. I didn't like doing it any more, I was afraid someone would report me because I'd been there so often, but I felt sorry for Hephzi. She had to rely on me now for her social life and frankly I'm not much of a joiner. It had been nice spending time with her, but she disappeared as soon as she saw The Father standing outside the vicarage, arms folded, legs akimbo. I knew he was waiting for me.

He pinched the back of my neck hard as he propelled me into the house. From a distance no one would notice his hand on me, no one would ever see the mark underneath my hair.

'Where have you been?'

'At school.' The words came out as a whisper and I knew my lie convinced no one. Lifting me by the hair, he picked me up and threw me against the wall. My head clipped the ancient mirror hanging there and brought it crashing down, banging my shoulder painfully as it went.

'Don't lie to me,' he threatened, his fist poised. I smelled the whisky on his breath, saw the red eyes and florid cheeks. Cowering, my arms over my head, I waited for the next blow.

'Where have you been?' he demanded again. 'The truth of it.'

'At a friend's house.'

'Liar!' he screamed and I braced myself for the blows.

I needn't have bothered with the fabrications. He knew I didn't have friends and he knew all about my job, one of the local busybodies had spotted me and spilled the beans, and my pathetic attempts to worm my way out of trouble saw me tumbling in the force of his rage; drowning, wheeling, caught by a wave elemental in its power. I could only wait for the tide to abate and trust that I would soon come up for air. When he'd finished with me I crawled up the stairs. He'd hit me in all the places where bruises can easily be hidden: my torso, upper arms, chest, buttocks and thighs. And he knew I wouldn't scream. The whole thing was silent, almost balletic, the dance so familiar now that I knew how best to crouch, how to move a shoulder to deflect a blow aimed at my breasts, but most of all how to hold back the tears. At least this time he hadn't had his strap. Hephzi had always said she would hide it and maybe that had been her last gift to me.

Earlier he'd ransacked my room and found the money I'd saved from the job and hidden under Hephzi's mattress. So he relieved me of today's ten-pound note too and emptied the edition of Eliot's poetry out of my bag, grinding it with his foot on the floor, just to make sure I learnt my lesson. I crawled under my bed, shuddering, and then started to hum a quiet tune, deep down in the back of my throat. If I filled my head with that noise I wouldn't remember anything else, I could force the pain away and become invisible. He'd knocked my hearing aid off the screw attached to the side of my skull and I was glad that everything was even more muffled now, as if I were swimming underwater. I lay under the bed with the dust balls and odd socks and imagined drowning. The carpet dissolved and I let myself sink, further and further, deeper and deeper, just as Hephzi had on the day she'd died.

Hephzi

Before

Finally I make it home from the pub. I've run all the way from the bus stop and I'm out of breath, but Reb has been watching for me and opens the front door to let me in, at no small risk to either of us, as she tells me in her best bossy-boots voice. I tell her to shut it and we scamper up to bed fast. I decide not to bother telling her what a horrendous night I've had when I see her scowl.

'What are you wearing?' she asks, dropping her mouth open, in horror, I suppose.

'Stuff of Daisy's. Why?'

'You look like a slut.'

'Shut up! You sound like Mother.'

'No, I don't. And you do look like a slapper. Admit it.'

I nearly laugh hearing Reb say that word, she's obviously picked up something about how to be normal at last.

'Don't you dare laugh! Don't you realize how risky all this is?'

We're hissing our argument, she's sitting there in her bed, a little ball of malice, and I'm trying to get out of the clothes fast before someone comes in and I'm rumbled. I stuff them under the mattress, my heart still skipping from the run home from the bus stop and the sneaking upstairs. If he'd caught me I'd probably be half dead by now.

'I'm not doing that again.' Rebecca won't shut up.

'Doing what?'

'Lying for you. Sneaking around, opening doors in the middle of the night. You'll get caught and we'll be in so much trouble.'

'Don't be so bloody pathetic. Nothing's happened, has it?' I leap into bed and pull the covers up to my nose, the thudding boom of my heart still crashing in my ears. It feels so good to be back in my room. I never thought I'd say that.

'Anyway, what was it like?' she asks eventually into the silent dark. I'd had my eyes closed but was nowhere near sleep. The night's events flash through my head, stills from a crazy film: me puking, Daisy dancing with Craig, the bus journey home.

'All right.'

'Only "all right"? All that trouble for "all right"?'

'Oh, shut up. Mind your own business. Come next time if you're that interested.'

'No thanks.'

'So what are you going to do, then? Live here for the rest of your life with them?'

For a long time she doesn't answer, then her words surprise me.

'No way. I'm getting out of here. First I need my exams and then that's it. I'll be gone.'

I can't believe that she's finally realized that we can't stay like this forever. It's about time too. I've never heard Rebecca talk like this before; she's the quiet one, the one without opinions or ideas about the future. I've always led and she's always followed and I wonder where on earth she thinks she'll go and what she thinks she'll be able to do.

'I'll go where no one knows me, where I can find a job.'

'Yeah, right. And where will you live?'

'I'll find a flat. Or rent a room.'

'In your dreams.' I don't know why I have to be mean and stamp on her hopes but I just do. 'You'll never get a job, Rebecca. You're too boring. Boring *and* ugly. Who'd want to have to look at you all day?'

She doesn't reply then and I mouth a silent sorry into the room and lie awake for a long, long time, watching her wrestle with some private demon – the one who makes her cry nearly every night.

I'm dreading going to college on Monday morning and, for the first time since the first day, I sit next to my sister at registration. I doodle on my notepad, not looking up or around in case they're all laughing at me. Rebecca is quiet too and for a second I think I know how she feels here almost every day. But then she nudges me hard and I look up. Craig is standing by the desk and I feel the hot flush on my cheeks before I can do any-thing about it.

'All right?'

I nod. Swallow. Smile, sort of.

'What happened to you Friday night, then?'

'Oh. Um. I was there.'

'Yeah, you disappeared.'

I don't answer, just shrug. This is the longest conversa-tion we've had. I keep waiting for him to walk off but he doesn't.

'I was looking for you. We all went on clubbing at Chequers.'

'Yeah?'

I don't really know what I'm supposed to say.

'I thought you might be there.'

'Oh. Sorry.'

He shrugs, shoves his headphones back in and wanders off, and I turn to Rebecca, who's looking like she might vomit. I elbow her in her side and she sucks in her breath and buries her head back in her Maths textbook.

So I'm not finished, not yet anyway. Even if Daisy did tell him about me puking up maybe he wasn't bothered. There might still be a chance. I spend all day looking out for him but he must have bunked off again because I don't see him anywhere.

This is my sixth day at this college. So far I've learnt a lot.

I've learnt not to look bothered if a boy talks to you or smiles at you.

I've learnt to make my voice rise at the end of some of my sentences.

I know how to use a computer, just about, and how to check my emails and Facebook account in the college IT room.

I've learnt that flicking my hair is quite sexy, although I think I'd got that one on my own.

I've also learnt the names of characters in *EastEnders* and more or less what's going on in the storylines, just by listening carefully. I'm quite proud of this actually.

I know who Cheryl Cole is, and all the characters from *Glee*.

I know the people here are probably not my BFFLs.

I know never to repeat a single word I hear in the vicarage.

I know that I've got to lie every day and that I can never invite any of my new friends home.

It's pretty exhausting spending every moment of every day lying to someone or other. I'm either pretending at college or pretending at the vicarage. The only time I get to relax is in bed at night and even then Rebecca could easily ask me a question that might catch me off guard. The only thing that she doesn't know about me though is that my life is as crap as hers. That I find it all as hard as she does. Maybe she's guessed but I don't think so, she thinks it all comes so easy for me, that I'm Little Miss Normal. God, how could anybody growing up in this place with parents like ours turn out normal? That's what

I've been hoping college might teach me, instead of all the stupid Maths and stuff, and I wish Rebecca would work a bit harder on her normality skills too. I watched her walk past me in the corridor today, her backpack heavy on both shoulders, bent over and muttering to herself, her trousers too short and those awful bright-green socks emerging from her clumpy shoes. I wanted to run over and push her behind me, hide her from the stares. I see people sniggering all the time, I've had to watch it all my life and for a long time I think it hurt me more than it ever hurt her. I want to yell at them to get lost, to leave her alone, maybe shove them or hurt them so they'll know what it's like to be picked on. But Rebecca, it's like she doesn't even notice and doesn't even care, so that's why I've given up on her and I leave her to get on with it now. She can embrace Weirdsville all she likes, but she's not taking me down with her.

I hope Craig's in tomorrow and that he talks to me again. If he does I need to make the most of it this time and show him I like him. Maybe he'll ask me out on a date and take me somewhere nice, just the two of us.

The week drags though and he's barely there at all. I take the plunge on Thursday and send a friend request on Facebook during study time. We're not supposed to use the Internet in the sixth-form centre during study periods but nobody else takes any notice of the rule so I don't see why I should. I wait for him to add me, fidgeting in my chair, clicking the mouse every couple of seconds for the entire forty minutes, forty minutes which should have been spent trying to do my Physics homework. Our parents made us take these stupid subjects and I can't follow a word of it. Nothing. *Nada*. It goes through my head like sand through a sieve and I know the teacher can see it too. I haven't answered a single question right yet. I watch Rebecca struggling to understand, the concentration on her face makes her look odder than ever, and I want to scream at them that we hate it, that we didn't want to do it and that he made us. Instead I copy someone else's answers and keep my fingers crossed the teacher will keep on letting me get away with it if I smile nicely and hand my homework in on time.

Every lesson is like that. What do Rebecca and I want with Maths and Physics and Chemistry? He chose our subjects, he thought they posed the fewest risks, and guessed we wouldn't understand a thing. We might as well have been studying Martian. He gets a kick out of proving we're useless. Him and his poxy Theology degree from Cambridge, which as far as I can tell has been the high point of his life so far. Ever since then he's been chasing greatness, trying to prove he deserves the big time, but the Bishop doesn't rate him, I guess, despite the hours he spends licking his boots, and the rest of his life has been a ride on the helter-skelter of anticlimax. He should face facts: we're not going to be brain surgeons or scientists or Nobel Prize winners. Rebecca should be doing English, every chance she gets she's in the library like some timid little mouse, burrowing into a book, and I could have done something fun like Photography or Drama. Daisy does both and laughs when she sees me trailing off to Chemistry with all the geeks, as she calls them. I've a good mind to swap classes, he would never know, not if I was clever, and I'd get to have a bit more fun. But Craig is in Physics, that is if he's in at all, and Maths too. Daisy told me he wants to go to uni and that he got all As in his GCSEs. Never judge a book by its cover, Granny used to say. Looks like she was right there. But she'd disapprove of me hanging around, moping about Craig She was always on about how we should make something of ourselves, not just get married and have kids, but do something proper, something to make her proud. Never rely on a man, she said. Silly old thing. We had fun with Granny though, until our parents found out and that was that.

Rebecca

After

After he found out about my job delivering papers, after he stole my money and beat me black and blue, I didn't know what more I could do. He'd meant to put me back in my place and to prove again that he was the king and I a mere minion. Hephzi didn't agree. She told me to get out, and to do it right then and there.

It's the only way, Reb, she says. *Like I've always said, we've got to get out. Please hurry though, don't wait, you have to hurry because there isn't time to spare. I promise we'll go together this time, you and me, we'll go together and be free.*

At last she'd begun to talk to me properly, not just little words here and there. She was back to making me laugh and acting the fool and I was glad to have her near. It had been so long since her funeral, so long since they'd put her in that box and piled earth on her head. Three whole months without her. And now that she was really here, with me whether I called her or not, it made the minutes I spent in the vicarage softer, almost bearable. But she was angry too; she thought people should know what had happened and that I ought to tell. *I didn't want to die, Reb!*

she tells me, crying, her head nestled beside mine on the pillow, just like when we were little. *Why didn't they care?* she asks, and I have no answer good enough, my own mistakes clanging loud in my ears like the Sunday church bells. Her life had just been getting interesting, she said. She and Craig had made plans. She wanted to know why no one was bothered enough to find out the truth, why Craig didn't at least come to our window and call.

I'd given up asking those questions long ago. When we were little I'd thought about pasting a sign on Hephzi's back for people to see as we tramped up the road. *Help us!* it would say. *Quick!* But I knew better than to bother, that the ink would be trick and would disappear on drying; no matter how fast I re-wrote the letters they would only melt away, dissolving like snow on water.

There had been a chance, just one. I don't know what happened, that was time that I lost, but Hephzi says I had a fit when he hit me too hard at the top of the stairs and Mrs Sparks walked in and there I was writhing on the hall floor, jerking and twisting, spinning like a top. Before he could say the words 'devil' or 'possession' or strike up a prayer, she was on the phone for an ambulance – cool as a cucumber, Hephzi said later. I just remember waking up in the hospital and staring up at the lights. Whether it was heaven or not, I wasn't sure, but I was almost hoping it would be, if Hephzi was there too.

A nurse came in.

'Awake at last! What on earth have you been up to?

What a pickle you're in.' I read her lips. This was before my hearing aids and the sound of the world was just a faint sigh.

Of course I didn't answer. But I felt that there was some sort of chance. She had something fine in her eyes.

She took my temperature and wrapped a tight band around my arm, pumping it up, then letting it down.

'How about a drink?' she asked and I nodded and sipped through a straw.

'The doctor'll be round soon. But don't worry, you're safe.' She smoothed the hair from my forehead and that touch was so cool that I cried.

'Hey, hey!' she soothed. 'It's all OK. You'll be fine. We mend people here! We don't want tears.' And then, almost as I opened my mouth to speak, she brought the sledge-hammer down.

'Your dad's just outside. He's been ever so worried. Well, haven't we all? But I think you'll be good as new, you're a strong little thing, aren't you? A proper little fighter. I'll tell him he can come in, shall I, poppet?' Off she went with a smile and in came The Father.

'Don't say a word,' he breathed into my face, 'or they'll take you away.'

If they took me away I'd never see Granny or my sister again, so I sewed my mouth shut.

He didn't leave me after that. He sat and held the hand of the arm that wasn't in plaster up to my elbow and his nail dug a groove in my palm.

There was an answer for every question, an excuse for every word. I'd been mucking about and fallen down the stairs. (*You know, foolish horse play, they've been told to be careful, many a time.*) He didn't mention that he'd hit me at the top or describe how I'd tumbled from stair to stair like the funny plastic Slinky toy we played with at Granny's.

The day they let me go, sound booming everywhere around me now that I had the screws and the boxes to allow me to hear, he bought that nurse flowers and chocolates and a card. He held both her hands and she flushed pink as petals on a new summer rose.

That was when I was nine.

Most of all Hephzi wanted revenge. So far I didn't dare spill her secret but maybe one day, if my soul ever found a place to breathe, I would.

As for leaving, well, how could I? I had no job, no money and still no idea if they'd fall for the summer-school plan. I was going to have to try again with The Mother but when I spoke, she pretended not to hear.

Hephzi could get The Mother to do almost anything. I don't mean she could get her to set us free, unless the college debacle counts, or that she could make her call off The Father when he'd flipped. But The Mother would do other stuff if Hephzi nagged. Mainly she could get her to lie to him and cover for her. That's how Hephzi managed to see Craig; if it hadn't been for The Mother pretending not to notice anything, then maybe my sister would still be alive. I'm sure she knew Hephzi was sneaking out, I'm sure she rumbled her and turned her vacant eyes the other way because she was afraid of what Hephzi might do or say, like she's afraid of him. People are. Both of them have this way of looking at you which makes you wish you were invisible. Hephzi would do it to me all the time. If I disagreed with her or warned her or advised her she'd fix me with that stare, that curled lip, which demanded, *Who are you to tell me anything?* Because I had warned her. Lots of times. When I'd found out about what she'd been doing with Craig I'd told her she was mad, asking for trouble and was bound to get found out, but she'd sneered and snarled until I climbed back into my box. I'd told her once, after one of her escapades with Craig, that it made her just like him.

'What do you mean?' She'd stared at me, wide-eyed. Little Miss Innocent.

'When you bully me, when you won't listen to me. When you treat me like I'm a nobody. That's just like HIM.' I mouthed the final word at her as loud as I could in the night-time of our room, silently shouting to be heard.

'I'm not like that! Don't say that, Reb!' She cried and said she was sorry, but I knew she wouldn't be able to help herself. Hephzi thought she'd learnt how to survive.

Even though I'd posted the application I knew the summer-school idea would have to go. It had been stupid to even think it was a possibility.

What are you going to do, then? asks Hephzi, nudging me again. I tried to ignore her when she kept on and on at me but she was getting louder all the time.

'I don't know,' I told her, trying to be firm. 'Just be quiet and let me think.'

At this rate you'll be leaving in a shitty cardboard box, just like me.

I took a deep breath and thought about it again. It couldn't be that hard, I reasoned. All I'd need to do was pack a bag, raid The Parents' wallets and head for the town. From there I could take a train or a bus and lose myself in some city far away. If they came looking for me I'd just run again, and anyway, it would probably be more trouble than it was worth for them to hunt me down. He could simply dress himself in his grief and sorrow as he'd done before, suck up the condolences of the village and go about his business as usual. The Mother could be his whipping boy for a change, it would serve her right. And then maybe when I was free and safe I could let the truth out. That would show them.

But how would I live? It wouldn't be safe. And who would employ me? I had no skills or talents and who would want to look at me, day after day? I had nothing to offer.

Night after night these thoughts kept me awake, winding in my sheets. I hid under the blanket, playing invisible, while I planned and plotted, plotted and planned. Eventually I'd go to sleep and then the nightmares would begin.

The sound of the crying in the wall was getting louder too, just like Hephzi. The crying has been driving me crazy for years, since I was thirteen, but now all three of them are at it. I wished they'd be quiet, just for one single night.

In the morning when I awoke everything cleared again. I could see that none of my plans was possible; the shadowy light of the vicarage turned the future back to black. I would never trick them. Wherever I ran to they would find me. And so they knew that I would stay.

It was a Friday in April and almost the Easter holidays. I was dreading the break; for all I hated college, I hated the vicarage more. As usual I'd been keeping my head down, being careful not to sit beside anyone or to make myself known. Period six was Maths and my teacher was some new supply, covering for nice Mr Connor, who'd gone off sick. The supply teacher, Miss Peters, was what you would call officious; you could tell she thought we should count ourselves lucky to be in her esteemed presence by the way she mocked people who got answers wrong, as if it was all so simple and we were all so thick. She called on me today for answers again, having acquired some notion that I needed to speak up in class, as if ritual humiliation were character building. Usually I had some idea of an answer which I could hazard, but not today. In fact I hadn't been listening at all, I dozed and daydreamed in my chair, thinking of anything but the formula which glared at me, black and angry, from the whiteboard. And so when she picked on me I couldn't even manage a guess. I felt them all waiting, the air in the room thickening with expectation. My cheeks began to glow and I shrank into my jacket as I heard the sniggers start. I started to hum softly, hunching over my textbook; I didn't need to hear the laughter and the taunts or feel the pellets of paper fired at my back to know they were enjoying my discomfort. Eventually Miss Peters cleared her throat and got on with the lesson, but the tense edge to her voice didn't slacken and I knew she'd keep me behind. My lack of co-operation, she told me at the end of the class, was making her extremely frustrated. She saw no reason why I couldn't at least try to make an effort like the rest of the class. She wasn't going to pander to me and give me special treatment, either I bucked up or she would be contacting my parents and would have to ask them in for a discussion of my progress. She stepped back, startled when I interrupted, my voice loud with sudden urgency.

'No. Please don't do that. I'll do better. Please.'

For the first time I met her eye. She gazed levelly back.

'What exactly is wrong with you, Rebecca?'

Her voice was soft and I understood at once what she was asking. She wanted to know all the gory details, to be let in on the secrets of my family and my face; for some reason she thought the fact that she was my teacher gave her the right to stare at me like I was an exhibit in a freak show. I picked up my bag, swallowing everything I wanted to say and had been waiting to say for years. Turning to go, I paused.

'There's nothing wrong with me, Miss. Nothing.'

So that was Friday and I did not want to go back to that place again, not ever. Hephzi keeps telling me to act normal, to put on some lip gloss and to try to be nice. She reckons I need to get over myself and that all my problems are in my head. Well, she's changed her tune, because that's not what she used to think. When she was alive she would nudge me and whisper, 'They're staring at you,' or, 'Stand over there, pretend we don't know each other.' She knew what it meant to be me, she just didn't feel it like I did and like I always will.

I didn't think anything could get worse after that. I was sure I'd reached the lowest point possible and when I got back to the vicarage all I wanted was to crawl upstairs and sink into forgetfulness. But they were waiting for me again. His face was ghastly and The Mother bobbed there at his shoulder, flushed with anticipation. For a second I didn't understand, I couldn't think what it could be, and then I saw what he held in his hand. A glossy brochure, sheets of typed paper. I glimpsed my name on the large white envelope. He had the proof, there would be no need for a trial.

Hephzi

Before

By Friday Craig still hasn't added me on Facebook and I feel rubbish. I've got my period too and a massive spot on my chin. No way am I going to risk going to the pub tonight. Daisy told me I could sleep over at hers but I told her no, said we were going away.

'How can you be going away? Doesn't your dad have to do all his vicar stuff at weekends?'

'Oh yeah, he does. But me and Mum and Rebecca are going to our gran's.' See, I told you I could lie.

'OK. Your loss. See ya Monday.'

She flounces off and I jog to catch up with Rebecca and we walk home together for the first time in ages. I think about my lie to Daisy.

'Hey, Reb, remember when we used to go to Granny's?'

She nods. She hates talking about it.

'Why'd they stop us?'

Rebecca looks at me like I've just asked her the colour of grass or whether the world is really round.

'He hated her.'

'Yeah, but why though? What did she ever do?'

'Hephzi, don't be thick. She took us out for ice cream. She bought you a bra. She told us not to believe his lies. He couldn't stand it. And he thought she'd tell someone what he did to us, he knew it was only a matter of time.'

'I miss her.'

'Me too.'

It's raining and our jackets aren't up to the weather so by the time we get back we're both soaked. I go straight upstairs and lie on my bed, my stomach cramping and my wet hair plastered in soggy strands around my neck. Rebecca comes in and offers me a cup of tea. I shake my head.

'You should take your wet jacket off. And your jeans.'

She's right. The heavy denim is claggy round my thighs. But I shake my head again.

'What's the matter?'

I bury my head in the mattress and eventually she goes away and sits on her own bed, humming and muttering. I scream into the blankets, wondering if I'll ever be able to stop.

Before we started college I always used to just lie in bed when I had my period. Mother won't buy us sanitary towels so I'd stuff my knickers full of toilet roll, itchy cheap stuff, and just lie there until I felt better. It'd usually be a few days. All day today I've sat in lessons with my pants stuffed with loo roll praying that it would hold and I wouldn't leave a mess anywhere. My thighs are chafed from walking home like this. I cry into my mattress some

77

more. Rebecca sits down on the side of my bed and pokes me in the shoulder. I shrug her off.

'Here,' she says.

'Go away.'

'I got you something.' I turn and look. She's holding a sanitary towel and two painkillers.

'Where'd you get that?'

'Her drawer. Right at the back. It was the only one, sorry.'

I roll out of bed, grab the stuff and go to the bathroom to sort myself out. I splash my face with cold water and look in the small mirror. It's so cracked and clouded that it's hard to make myself out, but I can tell that I'm all blotchy and red-faced. Ugh. Sitting on the side of the bath I wonder what I'm going to do.

When Monday comes I do my best to put on a good face. It's been a miserable weekend but Rebecca did my homework last night so I could rinse my hair and clothes. I'm running short of things. I've worn everything I own twice already and soon Daisy will notice. I returned her stuff the other day and she just screwed up the top and jeans into a ball and stuffed them into her bag like it was nothing. Mrs Sparks sometimes brings us things and I hope she'll be round soon. Or I could go and see her, just to give her memory a little prompt. I've been wondering if she's guessed something's up. I need more sanitary towels, so on the way to school I persuade Rebecca to distract the chemist with one of her many ailments while I nick some. I'm not a good thief; I get nervous, especially when I think of what would happen if I were spotted. But I can't go back to using loo roll, or even wearing old rags in my pants, washing them out and hanging them to dry in the bedroom. They never got clean, the stains stayed put, dark reminders of the pain. For once Rebecca does quite a good job on the chemist and I'm out of the door and hurrying further up the High Street without her. We're going to be late for registration now but who cares? This time I don't wait for my sister, I can't let people see us together too much, and I hurry and sign in and go straight to the study centre; I have a free first thing, and want to check my messages. There are loads of Facebook posts and I scroll through them, reading what the rest of the college was up to while I was stuck in the vicarage with Rebecca and my parents. This weekend Rebecca and I did the usual chores and then did penance, kneeling on the cold stone church floor for six whole hours. That was our punishment for failing to answer his questions about his sermon to his satisfaction. I wonder if I should post that as a status update.

But my heart lifts when I see that Craig has finally accepted my friend request and that he's sent me a private message. Blushing and grinning I click on it.

Where were you this weekend? You missed a good night. Party at mine
this Saturday. Be there.

I think I might be sick. This is the most exciting thing ever. I'm going to that party if it's the last thing I do, which if my father finds out it probably will be. This has to be proof that Craig likes me as much as I like him. It has to be. Daisy appears at my shoulder and I can tell she's straining to look at my screen. I quickly minimize it.

'Hi!' She sounds happy to see me and I smile back at her.

'Did you have a good time at your gran's, then?'

I remember the lie quickly enough to answer without a pause, 'Oh, yeah, it was OK.'

'We had such a good night on Friday. You really missed out.'

I shrug, what do I care?

'Yeah, we all ended up back at Scott's – his parents were out and it was a bit of a party. His older brother was there too with all his mates. Oh my God, this one guy, Billy, he was like, so fit . . .'

I nod as she tells me her story, not really listening but thinking instead what I'm going to need to do to escape on Saturday. I gather that of course Daisy got off with one of the older guys and is seeing him this weekend. She's full of it and I'm glad, at least it means she's not after Craig any more and maybe I'll have more of a chance.

'So will you bring him to Craig's party, then?'

'What?' For a second Daisy looks unsure, then smiles widely, tosses her hair and shrugs. 'Maybe, if we can't think of anything better to do.'

I eventually go to class and sit daydreaming through the experiment we're supposed to be doing in Physics. Luckily I'm partnered with Jack and he's such a keeno that he's more than happy to do all the work for me. It's easy to keep him sweet. I only have to smile and he blushes to the roots of his hair. He probably fancies me, most science geeks are lucky if a girl gives them the time of day, let alone tells them how great they are, so I keep on ladling out the compliments and he keeps on doing the hard graft. I think the relationship's working well for both of us. Rebecca disapproves of course, she says I'm taking advantage and that it's OK to do it to her but I should have more respect for other people. She can be such a bore sometimes. No wonder she's got no friends.

Anyway, I find Samara and Daisy at lunch in the common room and they're bitching about Craig's party.

'So how come you got invited and we didn't?' Samara folds her arms and looks at me hard with her head tipped to one side.

I shrug. I actually have no idea.

'D'you reckon you could get us an invite, then?'

Again I shrug. 'I suppose I could ask.' I can't help the reluctance creeping into my voice and I know it's really obvious that I don't want to.

'Don't you want us there or something?' Now Daisy sounds mad, and that's the last thing I need.

'Of course I do, it's just that I'm not sure I know him well enough to, well, you know, ask for favours.'

'But Craig knows me!' Daisy is still cross. 'I'm not just any old person, it's not like you're asking to bring that mongy sister of yours, is it?'

For a moment my head reels and spins. I thought that Daisy was my friend. I thought she liked me. I don't know why this hurts so much, I knew what she thought, of course I did. But she shouldn't have said it. I can't laugh it off.

'You ask Craig yourself if you know him so well, Daisy.' I stand up, just about, and walk away. Sorry, Rebecca. That was the best I could do.

Crying in the toilets doesn't help much. I make it through the afternoon without talking to anyone and I can't look Rebecca in the face as we walk home. She thinks I'm still upset about the weekend.

'One day things'll be better, Hephz,' she says.

I manage a laugh. 'Oh, yeah? When's that?'

We're nearing the vicarage and she stops and stares up at the house. It looks meaner than ever.

'When they die. Or when we do, I suppose.'

She mutters the words quietly but her anger's like a storm.

I reach out and put my arm around her.

'Don't be daft. We'll be OK.' Suddenly I'm the one doing the comforting and I wish I could give her a hug, but if our parents spot us there'll be trouble. We go inside and get on with our chores – the dishes, the laundry, the never-ending homework – and then, just when we think we can relax, he summons us down. It's one of the nights he wants us to sit with him. I try staring into space, forgetting I'm there, but he won't leave me alone tonight. I kneel on the floor in front of him and he brushes my hair. I guess this is weird, it was sort of OK when I was little but now I wish he wouldn't. He quizzes Rebecca about college but her answers are monosyllabic and I silently urge her to say a bit more because I can feel his body tense behind me. The less she says, the more she winds him up, and he digs the brush more firmly into my head with each word she doesn't utter. I try to signal to her but she's not looking at me either. *Oh, Rebecca, save me, save me*, I scream in my head and suddenly she swings round to face us and sees him with his hand tight on my neck and the other hand ready to swing the heavy hairbrush at my skull. I see my horror reflected in her eyes and want to vomit.

'My Physics teacher told me I wasn't working hard enough,' Rebecca says, clear as a bell. 'I'll be in detention if I don't pull my socks up.'

He drops me and goes for her. The usual words. Failure. Shame. Maggot. Filth. I cover my ears and run from the room, upstairs to hide. I wish I wouldn't. One day I'm going to hide that hairbrush and the strap. I'm going to stop him in his tracks. But for now I let my sister take my beating.

What else has she taken for me over the years? What does he do to her while I run away and hide? Like millstones my parents grind at her, circling, pushing, relentlessly punishing her for sins we don't even know exist. When I stop to look I see that each year she is a little smaller, as if a little bit more has crumbled away. One day there may be nothing left, just dust motes dancing on a scrap of light. Who will catch me then? Who will save me when I fall?

Finally it's over and she inches up the stairs and across the hall carpet on her stomach, a dying moth. I help her up and on to her bed.

'I'm sorry,' I whisper. She nods and her eyes close. I can hear her heart pounding, see it fluttering against her ribs, but she gathers her clothes around her and buries herself in the blankets. She hides her body, even from me. I hate to watch her suffering and stare out of the window. He beats her harder than he would me and that's another reason I should never have asked her for help, but I sit beside her and stroke her hair. Blood has clotted on her scalp and I fetch a cloth and try to wipe it away.

He never says sorry. He just pretends nothing ever happened. We've never dared fight back, not yet. I know what would happen if we did.

I remember being twelve and Granny is there. They're fighting and shouting and he is holding Granny by the neck and screaming into her face, she's telling him to calm down, pleading with Mother to call the police, and then he shoves her into the wall and pushes her out of the vicarage so hard she falls on the step in a heap, and he slams the door behind her. I don't want to remember the rest.

Neither of us goes to college on Tuesday. Rebecca feels

too bad and I don't want to leave her alone. Usually he's clever with his fists and never leaves a mark where it might be spotted, but this time, well, he didn't seem to care. I think he was enjoying it too much to mind. He knows he can lie it all away, anyhow. He's done it before. I ask if I can get her anything but she says not. By lunchtime I'm bored hanging round our room with nothing to do, and with Rebecca who's lying mute in bed, so I sneak downstairs and poke around the kitchen for something to eat. As I'm rummaging Mrs Sparks bustles in.

'Oh, hello, dear.'

'Hi.' I smile even though I don't want to. Mrs Sparks is annoying.

'I've just been helping your father with the church arrangements for this month. He's popped out now. What are you doing at home? It can't be study leave already, can it? You've only just started up there!'

'Oh, I just wasn't feeling all that well this morning. Nor was Rebecca, she's up in bed.'

'Poor thing. Do you need anything? Your mother's out visiting, isn't she?'

I see a chance.

'Oh, yes, if it's not too much trouble.' I smile more honestly now. 'We're out of painkillers and Rebecca has an awful headache.' This is no lie. 'And we don't seem to have much in for lunch either.'

She needs no further directions and hares off to bring back supplies. She's amazingly quick, panting up the back steps with a Tesco bag full of goodies she's garnered from her own kitchen and another bag bursting with an assortment of clothes and other bits and bobs. She thrusts them at me.

'Here you are, dear. And you tell Rebecca I hope she's feeling better soon. Pop over any time, won't you?'

Barely pausing to thank her I run up to the bedroom with the booty, chucking the painkillers at Rebecca and emptying the bag of clothes. They flow on to the bed, manna from heaven, and I crow with delight as Rebecca looks on. I hear her tear open the carton of juice and take a big gulp and I stop worrying about her and start planning my outfit for Saturday night.

I feast on the contents of Mrs Sparks' fridge and then we spend the afternoon lying on our beds, talking. Rebecca and I can talk forever and I doze off as she tells me one of her stories, the late autumn sun risking its last rays in our direction. I dream about the party, the dress I'm going to wear, about tripping up and everyone laughing, Craig kissing Daisy. When at last I wake I'm glad none of it really happened, but I feel trebly nervous now and confide in Rebecca.

'There's no way you can go.' She folds her arms and sits up straight.

'Why not?' She can't spoil this for me, but I know she's going to have a damn good try.

'Because the likelihood is you'll get caught. How many times do I have to explain this to you?'

'I didn't get caught before.'

She makes a noise which is a cross between a snort and a scream.

'That's because I helped you! I'm not helping this time. You're on your own.'

'You have to help me.'

'No, I don't.'

'Yes, you do.'

This could go on for hours. We're both stubborn but because I still feel bad I let the argument lie, for once letting her win, and change the subject.

'Are we going back to college tomorrow, then?'

She's still angry and won't answer. I leave her stewing and go downstairs; being late to the table is a cardinal sin and I hear Rebecca shuffling behind me. He won't mention what he did yesterday, he'll act like nothing's happened and we all will too. Maybe we should tell someone about him, we can't go on like this forever, and I try to remind myself to ask Rebecca later what she thinks. We could tell a teacher or Mrs Sparks and then, if we could make them believe us, it would all have to stop and we'd be safe. I look at our mother and wonder what would happen to her if we told. She might get in trouble too, or she might deny having anything to do with it. She's a good liar. The clock ticks loudly as we eat in silence. I feel Rebecca's fear like a vice round my belly and know that time's running out.

Rebecca

After

I wouldn't be going back to college. I crouched on the landing, holding the banisters and straining to hear as he made the phone call and told them that I'd decided to quit my studies. By the time the Easter holidays were over no one would remember that I'd ever existed, that's what he told me later.

If I didn't go back to college then that meant no exams, which meant no qualifications, which meant no job. Which meant no escape.

No!

Yes.

OK, then, just give up. Just stay here and die, if that's what you want. First it was Granny, then it was me. And you're next, Rebecca, Hephzi sneers. But I'd seen what happened if you tried to get out.

He'd opened my envelope, the one with the letter offering me a place at the summer school, he'd discovered everything and then he'd smashed it all to smithereens. I wondered if it was possible for the punishments ever to end. One day I must surely grow too old or bold to remain an object of tyranny. I was almost seventeen.

It was April, nearly Easter, and we were so busy. Ostensibly I was on tea and toilets, but behind the scenes there were other parts for me to act. I was Vice to his Justice and as he directed his very own morality play I felt the scorch of his flame again and again. As I cowered my mind hung on all the books I'd never get to read, all the stories he was keeping from me. It wasn't fair. Why should I have to stay in his prison, why should everything I'd ever loved be taken from me? If only I could get away. But how? It was impossible. If my sister had failed, my beautiful sister, then I had no chance. There was no one now who might help me.

For a long time I used to fantasize about moving to live with Granny or Auntie Melissa and Uncle Simon. My aunt and uncle were there at Hephzi's funeral, back at the start of the year, almost four months ago, and I guess they drove away with a sigh of relief on their lips. Maybe I should have spoken to Auntie Melissa when she'd tried to talk to me. Their names are never mentioned and they haven't tried to see me since. I suppose I don't blame them for staying away, it's dangerous interfering in what goes on in this house. Look at what happened to Granny.

The Father had stopped me from living for almost seventeen years, but he couldn't stop spring from coming and day by day I watched it. It was tempting me out. I pulled the heavy curtains in the back room a little to one side to see the tree blossom, big candles of cream and yellow dressing the garden ready for summer. The grass was growing, green and wild, and I hoped he'd let me out to cut it soon so I could smell the fresh scent and feel the sun on my skin. In the bathroom mirror I looked paler than ever and wondered if I might lift off sheets of skin and peel like ancient paper. I guessed my body would crumble to dust before the ink of my future had the chance to dry.

The clock ticked so slowly even though there was so much to do. I had to keep on my toes. Perhaps he'd test me; he liked to ask me questions to be certain I had been listening to his sermons, and there were a lot of them right then.

I was sick of listing sins. I was sick of repeating his mantras.

Other days I worked for The Mother; they pushed me between them like a mouse between two cats.

There was no way to protest so I draped myself in the garb of The Mother's misery and set to with the scrubbing brush and bleach. We had to get everything spotless, Easter is a big deal and there are usually visitors. She has been cleaning all her life but this house never changes. Dirt is ingrained in its pores. Still we scrub every day, harder, longer. I wondered what would happen if one day she were to awake and find every surface shining as if it were freshly made? Perhaps, the spell lifted, she'd smile and break free, fling open the front door and run off through the green garden to be swallowed up by the sun. Or maybe she'd vanish in a puff of smoke, or melt into a puddle on the polished parquet floor. I dunno. We only do downstairs and the church. I'm not allowed in their room, and she won't come into mine. Not after what happened. I'm glad she keeps out, it's better like that. And if she saw the wall now, if she knew what was hiding in there and growing bigger every day, she might hurt us all over again. She can't look after a child – you certainly couldn't trust her with a baby.

Usually we wouldn't speak as we worked. In fact, I couldn't remember our last conversation. Then suddenly, early on Good Friday, she started.

'Why did you do it? Why did you lie?'

It took me a long time to think of the right answer and even then it was wrong.

'I knew you wouldn't let me go.' I kept my voice low, I didn't want him to hear us.

'Of course not, you betrayed us. You're a sneak who can't be trusted, just like your father's always said.'

'I just wanted something else . . . I can't stay here forever. It was a chance to try something new.'

'You lied. The story about church camp. It was all a lie.' I nodded.

'I was going to ask for you. I thought you might go.'

She was the one lying now and I stopped following her lips and trying to hear.

'You're a wicked creature, Rebecca.' She stood up to leave. 'It should have been you.'

My parents have their own special definition of good and bad. In the Church our father's a man of God, round about the village he's a paragon of virtue, and in the vicarage I was evil because I had been marked. That's what they told me as soon as I was old enough to understand.

Later that day I sat in the church, beside The Mother. The Good Friday service had begun and it would be long. I didn't want to listen to a word he said. His theme was pride and I'd transcribed his nonsense for him and heard the words a hundred times.

'The proud are the devil's trumpeters!' he declaimed. 'When the Lord Jesus died on the cross, for all of you sinners, the Sin of Pride was defeated. But the pride of an ungrateful child is a thorn in the side of the Lord our God . . .'

I dropped my eyes and tried to vacate the present.

But the only memory that came to me was one of the saddest I have. When Granny died they took us to see her body lying in that cheap coffin, dressed in her old pink nightie. I wanted to kiss her goodbye. The room was terribly cold and the flowers which stood and nodded their sad heads in the vases on the sideboard would soon die too. The bruise on Granny's forehead was green and yellow and her face had fallen away. She'd had such a lovely smile and liked to pull funny faces to make us laugh.

Before we'd got there I'd been crossing my fingers and hoping that it might not be true and that my granny might still be alive after all. Someone could easily have made a mistake, I thought. I stood watching, straining to hear her breathe.

It was pointless. She looked so much older than she had when we'd last seen her. Old and defeated and sad. She had gone. And I knew that she died because he wouldn't let her love us, I knew she died because he shut her out. Whatever they said about her falling down the stairs, I knew it was his fault really.

I jolted out of the memory when Hephzi yells in my ear to stand up for the readings, everyone else was already on their feet and he was staring at me and waiting.

After the final prayers I followed The Mother from the church, back to the vicarage, and took one last gulp of the world outside as she shut the doors behind us.

I cry for Granny and for Hephzi late at night when no one can hear. I wouldn't cry at their funerals, even though I knew it made me seem odd, because I never let The Parents see my pain. I keep my hurt hidden, remember?

I woke early on Easter Sunday, before I was even needed. I wanted to talk to Hephzi and give her my gift. I'd always given her something on our birthday. This year it was a flower. A snowdrop I'd picked months ago, so fragile that I cradled it in my hands as if it were made of dreams. I'd pressed it for her and saved it all this time, hidden in the floorboards. I placed it on her bed and waited.

Soon we were back in the church to make sure everything was in order. The bells were ringing and it was sunny and bright outside but the green day receded as we shut the door behind us. By the time the service started I felt like sleeping; I hid my yawns behind my hands and pretended to pray. He was hoping for a good turnout and had been composing his sermon for weeks. I knew I should quit prodding and poking at the scars on my heart but I couldn't stop myself from drifting off again into the past, although it's not always safe there either.

The last time we had seen our granny had been on our twelfth birthday.

We're seventeen today! Hephzi cries. I nodded and told her to hush.

Back on that birthday Granny arrived early to collect us and The Mother let us go with her, nervously twitching at her blouse and reminding Granny over and over again to be back before four. We'd only been allowed to go in the first place because Hephzi had cried and pleaded and thrown the biggest tantrum I'd ever seen.

Granny reassured The Mother that she would bring us back safe and sound. 'Of course I will, you silly thing. Now go and get some rest, stop all this rushing about. I'll look after the girls, you know I always do.'

We'd run down the drive with her holding our hands, she'd been beaming at Hephzi and then at me, laughing at nothing.

She'd asked what we wanted to do and Hephzi had

chosen first, so of course it was the shops. I remember touching the clothes, holding the dresses up against my body, smelling their newness and inhaling excitement. Granny had bought me a T-shirt with Minnie Mouse on it, grey and red. Even Hephzi said it was nice. We'd gone to the underwear department then and Hephzi had chosen her first bra and new pyjamas.

'Your turn soon, love,' Granny had said to me, but I wasn't jealous. I didn't want to grow like Hephzi; I didn't want The Father's eyes to fix on me like they fixed on her.

After that we stuffed ourselves with burgers and chips and cake and ice cream. I crammed the food into my mouth so fast that Granny looked worried and told me to slow down, I would be allowed as much as I liked. Even though I felt sick I kept going, as if the flour and sugar and sweetness would fill the hole in me that was growing so fast I was afraid it would swallow me up.

Our twelfth birthday. Hers were the only presents we received; hers was the only kiss, the only smile, the only laughter. I chose the bookshop for my treat and we sat in there for ages. I pulled out a pile and surrounded myself with stories. I could have stayed there all night. Granny laughed and bought me two new books to stay at her house, waiting for me when I next came, heavy hardbacks with glossy covers which I carried carefully, like treasure or a stick of dynamite.

Then there was the film, our joint request, but it was longer than Granny had realized and when we left the cinema, sticky from popcorn and fizzing with sugar, it was already a quarter to four.

'Don't worry girls, Granny'll get you back safe and sound,' she'd said, hurrying us through the car park and into her little Mini. I remember how she'd driven, jerking through the gears, her foot revving the accelerator and her head craning forward as her teeth gnawed her lip. Hephzi and I were quiet in the back, we'd not even fought over who should sit in the front, and I stared at the clock on the dashboard, willing it to slow.

But he was there when we returned, waiting. I'd wanted to tell Gran to just drop us off at the bottom of the drive, but she'd parked and, determined, followed us inside.

'What's all this?' He was ready.

'Roderick, how are you?' Her voice sounded normal except for a little quaver as she said his name.

'Where've you been? Have you any idea of the time?'

'Yes.' She was still calm. 'It's half past four. We've had our lunch and had a nice day. Now the girls are back safe and sound. They'll be ready for their tea soon.'

'Who gave you permission to take my daughters out of this house?' He made a step towards her.

Hephzi was already on the stairs, she'd slunk round the back of him, ready to run. The bag, containing the bra Granny had paid for and the pair of pink frilly pyjamas she'd had as an extra present from me (Granny had passed me the money in secret and winked, my co-conspirator in the plot for Hephzi's happiness), was clutched to her chest. The hallway smelled of danger, like spilt wine and burned flesh. The Mother was standing in the doorway to the kitchen, a tea towel wrapped round her arm.

'Thanks for a lovely day, Granny!' I turned to my gran, copying her pretence at civility. I could do normality, given the chance.

'You're welcome, my love, my birthday princess.' She bent to kiss me but I felt a hand in my hair and was dragged out of her reach.

'Stop that! Don't you do that!'

I tried to find Granny's eyes with my own, to beg her to save me and to warn her to be silent, but her gaze blazed at The Father as she stepped towards him. The top of her head came barely level with his chest, she was hardly taller than Hephzi, but she squared her shoulders and stepped towards him again. He started to laugh.

'Get out of here, you stupid old cow. And don't come back.'

'I won't leave. Not until you promise me you'll start treating these girls properly. I don't like what goes on in this house, it's time it stopped.'

'Get out, I said,' he screamed into her face, menacing her now, forcing her backwards.

'You change your ways or I'll be taking steps. I promise you that, Roderick.'

He gripped her neck and shoved her hard into the door. 'Shut your face.' His finger prodded at her face, furious, frantic. 'Shut your bloody face and keep out of this family. They're nothing to do with you.'

'I'm their grandmother. I have a right.'

I willed her to stop arguing. She should stop fighting and save herself, but she was too brave. I turned to The Mother, pleading with my eyes, but she turned her back and slunk off into the kitchen, leaving them to it.

'Please don't hurt Granny,' I tried. 'She didn't do anything, honestly.'

That finished it for her. I should have kept my mouth shut but I'm stupid like that, always making things worse, and he threw her out of the door and on to the step, slammed and locked the door, barricaded it with his body and turned his face towards me.

Saliva hit my cheek as he snarled his hatred and spattered me with his disgust.

After that she disappeared from our lives; he made her vanish as if she were a genie forced back into its bottle. All that remained were a few whispered conversations on the telephone and once I found her Christmas card before he had the chance to destroy it. Her handwriting was faint and wavering, as if without Hephzi and me she was gradually disintegrating.

She never came back.

The Mother nudged me out of my dream and I stood again to say the final prayers. There were more people around than usual and The Father was standing by the altar handing out chocolate eggs from a basket to the little children who clustered around him with outstretched hands. I'd never been entrusted with the basket; my face would frighten them. But Hephzi had liked doing that job and he'd let her.

She stole one once; it was around the time of our tenth birthday. I saw her unwrap it with nimble fingers and stuff it whole into her mouth and then watched as her face dissolved in ecstasy. We both realized at the same time that The Mother had seen her too. I thought for a second that Hephzi would cry, but she didn't, she grabbed another egg, peeled off the glinting foil and popped it into our mother's open mouth, making her complicit in the sin. The Mother didn't spit it out. And she didn't admit it later when he counted them up. Guess who got the blame?

And now I was trapped with him in the vicarage.

Happy Birthday, Hephz, I whispered at the end of the day. She didn't answer. But the wall behind her bed shifted and moaned.

Everything went quiet after Easter. No one in particular visited the vicarage and I didn't go out. I counted the hours and did as I was told, hung my head in shame and learnt my lines well; I trod a path of pain and he laid down new scars on my heart. Whenever I could I played the invisible game and pretended I didn't exist.

Every now and then Mrs Sparks popped in and it was always a relief to see her. They hated her coming but she never got the message and just kept on turning up, surprising us all. When she was there he had to be nice.

She's what they call a churchwarden and she bustles about, lists in hand, pen at the ready, on call to do service wherever and whenever she can. I've known her all my life. Mrs Sparks likes The Father. He impresses her with his long words, pontificating about God and His wishes for His flock. She flirts with him, smoothes her hair and offers to do the flowers for the church even when it's not her turn. She has no idea. Anyway, she cottoned on to the fact that I'd left college pretty quickly once all the other kids in the village went back to start the summer term at the tail end of April, and her sharp eyes fastened on me as I quietly brought her sweet tea. She raised an eyebrow.

'Why aren't you at college, Rebecca? It's exams soon, surely?'

I didn't dare answer her.

'I'm sure you're terribly useful around the vicarage, dear, but really, it's a terrible burden on your parents, having to keep you at your age. Really if you're not going to bother with your studies you ought to find a job.'

The Father nodded and pretended to agree with her assessment, protesting that I was too shy even to try, but the next thing I knew I'd been let out on day release. Thank you, Mrs Sparks.

Instead of living out the rest of my existence in the vicarage, I was to go next door.

The care home next door is a place for all the people no one wants any more. If you lollop and your face is twisted, if your voice comes out slurred and you can't really hear, if you're old and have forgotten how to remember, then that's where you'll end up. And that's where I was going.

'You'll fit right in,' he said when he told me, late that night as I lay in bed, before he laughed and slammed the door.

At first it was hard. The smell of hours lived out in lingering resignation stayed on my clothes and I carried it back with me to my room at the end of every day. I didn't like to look at those faces; I don't want to feel the way I know people feel when they see me.

Hephzi wouldn't come, she told me so, there was no way she was setting foot in that place.

It stinks of piss, she says, *and those weirdos freak me out.* I sighed and went off alone. Anywhere was better than the vicarage.

On my first day the woman in charge, Mrs Sweet, handed me cleaning stuff and I set to work in the bathrooms. It was hard work and I tried to daydream as I scrubbed the dark yellow stains from around the rim of the toilet bowl. Remembering where I was up to in *Middlemarch* before The Father ripped it up kept my mind off the past and I finished the story in my head. The stench and the stains on the loos refused to be masked but at least I didn't need to fear footsteps in the hallway, adumbrating pain. By lunchtime I was sweaty and stinky; I would have to try to sneak to the chemist and steal a deodorant, like Hephzi had done. I could just imagine her pulling faces at me and holding her nose when I got back later. The carers ate with the residents in the sunny day room and I felt my stomach knot up as I watched the messy business get underway. I looked them over, for once I was the one doing all the staring, and it was strange to see these people, their faces creased with life, wearing plastic bibs and sipping through straws held by patient, younger hands. Guiltily I looked down at my plate and shuffled the bits of salad. I couldn't eat the soup, not when I'd watched it slide down so many faces and be mashed into so many fists.

I didn't mind the work. It was easier there than in the vicarage. The Parents were leaving me alone and although I didn't trust their silence it was a relief. The pattern repeated itself, day in, day out. I cleaned, I wiped, I helped to dress and change and feed. Hephzi still kept away when I was there and I didn't really blame her. No one really talked to me, although they smiled. The other carers and cleaners were mainly foreign workers, from Eastern Europe or the Philippines, but it didn't matter if they didn't understand the residents since none of them made any sense anyway.

It was another Friday but I wouldn't be going out, I was in my room and it was almost clean. I knew the stains had been growing and I'd been avoiding looking at them, but it was getting so that if I didn't at least try to clean them away then they might burst. The hoover belched and groaned and once I'd cleaned the floor I scrubbed at the marks on the walls by Hephzi's bed. They wouldn't come off even though I used bleach. Even as I worked it seemed they were growing, bulging like pregnant bellies over the paint she'd hopefully slapped on the wall.

You're going barmy, Reb! Hephzi laughs and I nodded and tried to think of other things. But they stayed in the corner of my eye wherever I moved. I hoped I would not be here when they exploded. Hephzi laughs when I explained. She tells me to grow up and stop being such a scaredy cat.

It's only damp, silly, that's all, she claims.

But I didn't want to see her baby. I didn't want to see it lying there on the floor, like jelly, no eyes or mouth. I knew I had to get out – the house was full of ghosts.

On Friday nights Hephzi used to sneak out. It was her big night out with Craig, every week. She wouldn't come back until the early hours; I'd know because I'd be awake, waiting and worrying. When Hephzi was alive I didn't want a boyfriend, the thought made my insides curdle, but now. *Now*. Maybe I could find someone. Someone who could look at me and see more than my face.

Hephzi used to climb out of the window; it's a cliché but it worked for her. There's an obliging old tree that bends near our room and she somehow found a way of getting down without breaking her neck. Craig would wait on the road just outside the vicarage and she'd jump on the back of his moped and I'd strain to hear them putter off up the High Street. I moved over to the window and pushed up the bottom sash. I leant over and looked out. The night was still and quiet and I breathed in the fresh sweet air and caught the half-light on my face.

How did Hephzi manage to be so brave? How did she risk it, night after night? I ask her to tell me, to give me some of her courage and some of her heart, but she won't say a word.

Gingerly I climbed up on to the sill, hoping the window wouldn't fall and guillotine me in two. I used to hold it tight for Hephzi. For a long time I sat there, half in, half out. When it was really dark and getting cold I climbed back inside and sat on my bed, staring at the bulging wall opposite.

Hephzi

Before

The next day I make it in to school although Rebecca's still too poorly. She'll have to stay in the vicarage until she's fit to be seen. But one of us has to go to college, Mother says, or there might be talk. I feel guilty for feeling free as I bomb out of the house and up the road in record time. Craig is there by the gates, smoking, cute with his hat pulled down over his forehead. I slow down, matching cool with cool.

'All right?' he asks as I get closer. With a flick of my hair I shoot a quick smile in his direction and keep walking as if I'm going to go past without pausing to chat. Craig moves into my path to stop me and I realize how tall he is now we're so close and I look up into his eyes, which are as dark and sexy as I'd imagined.

'Hi!' Where did that voice come from? I sound like a little girl.

'Where are you off to in such a hurry?'

'Registration?' I inflect my voice, grinning with my eyes but making a face of mock disapproval.

'Waste of time. Let's get out of here.'

This is it. Crunch time. It had to happen sooner or later, he had to find out that I'm a total loser. Any other day and I'd have been out of that school like a shot, but if I disappear now and my parents find out then Rebecca will be punished again. Me too. On the other hand I know that if I don't go with him this time then Craig probably won't bother asking in future. This could be my only chance. He smiles a little smile and touches my waist. I'm on the verge of capitulating.

'Sorry, I have a test. Can't miss it.' Reb's asked me to get the homework for her too.

He steps back, shrugs, looks over his shoulder and is already gone, loping off, destination anywhere but the science block. I force my legs to carry me in the right direction and flunk the test.

But when I check Facebook at lunchtime there's a message. Craig.

Hope you won't bottle it on Saturday.

I guess that means he's still interested. I confide in Samara and she agrees and says I did totally the right thing.

'Treat 'em mean, keep 'em keen, girl. That's what it's all about.'

Nodding, I store that one away for future reference. I thought I'd learned most of the rules, seems I still have a long way to go. After lunch we both have free periods and I go back to Samara's, she puts on MTV and I make mental notes. Daisy's clearly watched some of these videos way too many times; I remembered her dancing in the pub. She has all the right moves and all the right clothes. All the swagger. I sigh. Craig will never look at me while she's around. Samara says that's not true and that I'm just as pretty. I can't help but smile. I've always wanted to have a friend and it feels better than I imagined, rich and warm in my tummy and throat, like the hot chocolate Granny would give us after we'd been to the park. Samara's mum bustles in and out with drinks and snacks. She grins widely at me and invites me back; apparently if I'm the vicar's daughter then I must be a Nice Girl, not like Daisy, who's a Bad Influence. That's what Samara whispers to me as I leave in a flurry of further invitations. We giggle and I swing my bag on to my shoulder, promising to see about asking Craig if she can show up at his party, and head off, feeling better than I have in ages.

Floating home I don't notice anyone's walking to catch up with me until it's too late. He grips my arm, that tight grip I know so well and I swing round to face him.

'Not staying behind at school tonight, Hephzibah?'

I shake my head. What is my father doing, trailing round after me, creeping up on me in the street?

'I've been out, doing my visits, there are a lot of people in this village who need me, you know, Hephzibah.'

'I know.'

'Indeed. Well, it's strange. Perhaps you can help me to clear up a bit of a mystery?' His voice is cool, a dangerous, dark pool into which I could topple without a trace.

'Yeah?'

'Someone said they'd seen you last weekend, last Friday night, in fact. Wandering the streets.'

'What?'

'Well?' His grip tightens and I try to pull away. His face is grim. 'I certainly hope I can trust you, Hephzibah.'

'T-they must have been mistaken,' I stutter.

'If I choose, I can soon put paid to your little college ambitions. You'd be wise to remember that, wouldn't you?'

I nod. He releases my arm but stays too close, walking almost so our shoulders touch. I think he's finished but he starts up again.

'What I mean to say is, just to be precise, I don't want to hear any more stories about a daughter of mine behaving like a whore.' He leans in on the final words, hisses them into my ear. I nod frantically, desperately.

Rebecca hates him but, because he's been a bit less harsh to me, I can pretend not to. I do what I do to survive. Even if that means acting like the worst of what he does isn't really happening. I'm not strong like Reb, but she's stupid, too. You can see the loathing coming off her in radioactive waves and he gets her for it, time and again.

'I hope you're studying hard.' I swallow and nod. 'Your mother was no good at school. She didn't need to be, she married me. Women's ambitions are best served in the home, Hephzibah. It's a modern world and people expect modern attitudes, but personally I think old ways are best. Don't you agree?'

His conversational tone is just as dangerous as his threats and I pick up my pace. He matches me easily.

'I said, don't you agree?'

'I suppose so.'

'So we'll have no more of this nonsense.'

'Oh, but I really want to finish the year. Please.' I make my voice soft and wheedling and try one of the smiles that usually help me get my way.

'We'll see.'

My only chance of getting out is about to vanish. Panicking, I think hard for reasons to justify what I'm saying.

'People will think it's weird if we drop out just after we've started. This is only my third week! And I am learning a lot, I promise. Stuff that'll be really useful. Imagine how proud you'll be of me when I get good results!'

He sucks in air between his teeth and thank goodness we're back at the vicarage before I get myself into any more trouble. I run ahead and upstairs to see Rebecca, who looks glad when I slam in. Her face is still swollen but a bit better than it was, and her smile is more real.

'Good day?'

'Yeah, great.'

'How was the test?'

I wave a hand in dismissal. 'Flunked it for sure. But I don't care. Craig was waiting for me this morning.'

'What?'

'Yeah, he wanted me to cut school with him.'

'What?' Her voice is an octave higher. 'You didn't, did you?'

'Nope. But only because of *you*.' I give her a hard look and she nods and sinks back on to her bed.

'Next time, I'm out of there though, quick as a flash, that I can guarantee. There's no time to lose, Reb, I mean it. You Know Who followed me home, it's like he was trailing me or something, and then he started going on at me about college and how girls should just stay at home. All that crap. Anyway, he's going to try to stop us going. So I need to find a way out, and fast. This is my only chance.'

There's a long pause which I barely register until she speaks again in a voice so small I hardly hear it.

'And what about me?'

I exaggerate a huge sigh. Hands on hips, I stand over her.

'God helps those who help themselves, Rebecca, surely you know that by now?'

She manages a giggle and I sink down beside her.

'Seriously though, sis, you need to think what you're going to do. You can't stay here forever. It's not safe. He'll kill you one of these days.' She grips my wrist tightly.

'I know. I know. But how can I leave? Where could I go?'

'Start working on it.'

'Well, what about with you?' She sounds tearful. I squeeze her hand gently.

'That'd be fine with me, Reb, you know that, but I don't even know how I'm getting out yet, do I? So I can't make any promises. It's best if we both have our plans.'

'Why don't we leave together? Just run away?'

'With what money? We've got nowhere to go and I don't want to be some kind of homeless runaway living on the streets. No. We've got to have help. You need to start thinking about that.'

'You don't have to rely on a boy, you know.'

'At least it's a plan. It's better than nothing.' I pause and decide to defend myself. 'And I'm not totally relying on him, I just really like him. OK?'

She shrugs, I know she thinks I'm pathetic but she's just as bad. She won't do anything to help herself. But I can't have her hanging on to me, relying on me. I can't manage everything for both of us. I can't even manage just for me, that's why I need Craig's help. I'm scared to do it all on my own.

After a while she pipes up, 'You need me just as much as I need you, you know.'

I don't bother answering. Just let her see how wrong she is.

Craig's party is causing me serious worry though. Not only do I have my own twin sister refusing to help me out but I also have my father breathing down my neck, watching me wherever I go. Or if not him, his spies. God knows who he's got reporting back to him. My teachers? My friends? I wouldn't put anything past my father. But if I don't show up I know I'll have blown it with Craig once and for all.

My mind spins in tiny circles trying to think of a way to go to the party. I get down on my knees to Rebecca but she doesn't budge. It's no use trying God, I don't think he's listening to us. Like I told Reb, you've gotta help yourself.

Maybe I could get Samara to invite me to stay over, then get her mum to phone and speak to my mother and tell her that I'm invited there and staying the night. But I don't know how to float this idea with Samara and I'm worried about what I might have to say to get her to help. There are way too many things that could go wrong with that plan, she might want to come here or something and no way could that happen.

I speak to Mother on Thursday evening after spending the whole day stressing out over what to do. Saint Roderick's out at a parish council meeting and there's no chance he'll interrupt us. I corner her in the kitchen. She's wiping round, tidying up, busily distracted as always. It's cold in the kitchen even though it's been warm for late September and I shiver. She doesn't want to sit still and listen to me but I push her into a chair.

'Look. This is how it is.' I tower over her and although her eyes look defiant I know I can make her give in. If I didn't think I could make her help me then there'd be no point even trying.

'I beg your pardon?' She crosses her arms. Blinks rapidly.

'I have to go out on Saturday night. I need you to sort it.'

'You can't go out.'

'Yes, I can. Because if you don't make this happen then I'm telling.'

'And what do you mean by that?' Her sharp eyes open wide and look at me dead on. I know she's jealous of me, but I'm still her favourite. She wouldn't give Rebecca the shit off her shoe. Favourite's the wrong word actually; I'm just the one she hates least. Things might be better between us if he didn't keep pestering me, I know that's what winds her up, but it's not like I encourage him, even if that's what she thinks. It's not as bad as when I was younger but there's something about how he looks at me sometimes that makes me shiver. Even though he never does more than hold my hand or brush my hair, or make me sit on his knee. Yuck. I'm sixteen, not a little dolly. I don't pull away, that would only make it worse, and I'm never alone with him, Reb makes sure of that.

I go in for the kill.

'I'll be letting my teachers, and anyone else who wants to listen, know exactly what goes on in this house.'

Her chin juts out in determination. 'You wouldn't dare. Your father will sort you out.'

'No, he won't. If you don't do this for me, then I mean it, I'll make your life hell.'

She hasn't got a clue that I'm on the verge of peeing my pants I'm so scared. Blackmail, if that's what you could call it, is new to me but I'm desperate now and am willing to try anything. In the past I've manipulated her just by copying our father, shouting, stamping my foot, giving her the silent treatment or, if that doesn't work, shoving or pushing her around. I'm bigger than her and I'm stronger. She's nearly as thin as Rebecca. But I hope I won't have to resort to that. It makes me feel like him.

'What do you want me to do?'

She's given in too quickly and I eye her warily.

'Make sure he's looking the other way on Saturday night. Make sure I get in and out without him knowing.'

I wait for her to laugh in my face.

'How?' she says finally, her tone derisory.

'I don't know. Drink? Have sex? Pray? Whatever it is you two do together. I don't give a shit.' I've never said things like that to her before. The swearing wasn't planned but I reckon it added quite nicely to the overall effect. She goes green. 'Do we have a deal, then?'

Very, very slowly she nods and I step back from her, although she's in no hurry to rise. If she goes back on our agreement then I'm finished. Surely she can see that. The fact that I've trusted her to help me means she has to decide. Me. Or him. That's the choice.

After that the hours go slowly by. Thanks to Mrs Sparks' bag of goodies at least I have a half-decent outfit to wear, so I can almost relax about how I'll look. I nicked a new blusher from the chemist on the way home from school tonight and added it to my stash. Now I have one lip gloss, Mother's eyeshadow, the blusher and an old mascara I saw Daisy chuck in the bin in the girls' loos at school. I went back and fished it out and there's loads left in it, like I guessed. Daisy has everything and I try not to be jealous or at least not to let her see how much I covet her things. But she's still not really speaking to me after the whole row about the party invites and I haven't forgiven her for what she said about Rebecca, so I suppose she's not my friend any more. I'm guessing she'll show up anyway, Samara reckons so too; Daisy hates missing out on anything. We've been bitching about her a bit but I'm careful not to say too much, just in case. She and Samara have been friends forever and I don't know if I can trust her really, sometimes people don't mean what they say.

Craig will be different though. You can tell your boyfriend anything, that's how it works, and they tell you their secrets too. We'll do everything together. He'll be my new best friend and love me more than anyone ever has. It'll be like one of the books Rebecca reads. *Jane Eyre*, maybe, but he won't be blind and I won't be dull. Still, he'll love me in that sort of way – passionately, like he'd die for me if he had to. Perhaps we're more like Elizabeth Bennet and Mr Darcy. Mainly he has to help me get out, that's what Darcy did, he rescued Elizabeth from her awful family, and Craig can do the same, cos I'm darn sure I can't do it on my own and Rebecca's deluded if she thinks we could make it out there together on the strength of a few exams. I mean, I can't look after myself, let alone her as well. You have to know your limits; without money or qualifications I wouldn't get further than the next town, he'd chase me down and round me up and bring me back here quick as you like.

Craig's not a very romantic name. If he were called something like Fitzwilliam or Heathcliff, that would be better. But I'm not so superficial that something like that matters. He's cool and he's clever and he likes me. Those are the main things.

Rebecca's telling me to go to sleep now so I'm going to have to try to nod off, even though these thoughts won't leave me alone. I ask for a story and she tells the Darcy one again. Bliss.

Rebecca

After

The more hours I worked at the care home, the more I got paid. He couldn't ask them to pay him on my behalf so I was managing to keep some of my wages hidden. You'd think I would have learnt my lesson, but I wasn't a good student. Not any more. I'd found something else to be good at, you see. The people at the home were pleased with me, Mrs Sweet said I was a trouper, and I was beginning to realize that I might stand a chance. Like I'd always told Hephzi, we could do it on our own. Granny had said so too and she'd been right. When I made one of the residents grin, or was just in the right place just when I was needed, I knew I'd done well, I knew I wasn't useless. *Big deal*, says Hephzi, but it was to me.

I was sure The Father suspected I was saving but so far I was getting away with my little act of rebellion. He'd been drinking more and more and the atmosphere in the vicarage had been as viscous as the glue they used in the home when the residents did craft. Feathers, sequins, felt; I helped them to stick, and I swept the floor when they'd finished. The sight of them sitting in their chairs like a bunch of crazy kings and queens wearing glitter crowns made me smile.

In the morning as I left for work I pulled the door shut behind me and took great gulps of fresh air. The early summer was warm and sweet and I drank it up, running the hundred yards out of the drive and over the road to the home. It felt good to slough off the sticky skin of the vicarage. It felt good to be like a normal person. If I saw Mrs Sparks, I'd wave. The postman said hello to me and grinned. I could almost forget the nightmare I'd left behind me in my room. I tried not to worry about them all, stuck up there, crying and complaining; after all, I'd asked Hephzi to come with me to work and it was her choice to stay behind.

I was getting used to the folks at the care home too; they meant no harm and sometimes, if I waited long enough, one of them might open their eyes and look at me and for a moment I'd see who they might once have been. One old lady who was nearly a hundred had eyes the brightest blue. They shone in her face, sharp, blinking stars, and I knew she was thinking things she couldn't say. I sat and held her hand whenever I had a minute and she liked it, I could tell. Today I found a pile of books in the day room, someone must have donated them and they'd been plonked on a coffee table, just sitting there doing nothing. They weren't classics or anything special, but they were books none the less, stories, pages with words. I decided I was going to read them all. Maybe I would read them aloud to my new friend, I thought she might like it.

As I work I make plans. Danny, the chef, always laughs at me and asks me what I'm daydreaming about. The first time he spoke to me I blushed.

'It's all right, love, I don't bite!'

I dropped my eyes and inched away, but every so often I plucked up the courage to stop and talk to him a bit. He listened when I told him about Cyrilla, the blue-eyed lady, and said he would make sure he did her favourite more often. She couldn't really chew so we had to mash everything up, but I knew she liked his roast beef, roast potatoes and gravy best. She never spat that out.

'So, what's a nice young girl doing in a place like this, then?' Danny asked me as I was helping him with the veg for lunch. Somehow he had engineered it so that I had been moved off toilets and into the kitchen. It took ages, peeling, slicing, chopping, but it was definitely more fun than scrubbing the loos. I shrugged.

'How old are you, love?'

'Seventeen.'

'Well, shouldn't you be at college or something? My lad, Archie, he's just turned sixteen now, he's doing his GCSEs. He's planning on staying on after, getting some more qualifications. You don't want to spend your life chopping veg, do you?'

'No. I don't.' I looked guiltily around, hoping no one had heard me. I didn't want them to think I was being ungrateful.

'So? Get out there, get yourself to college, find something you like doing and go for it.'

'I tried. I wasn't any good.'

'What at?'

'Maths.'

He laughed. 'There's more to life than Maths, you know.'

'Not just that. The other kids, the teachers, they didn't like me. I didn't fit in.'

'Look.' Danny stopped what he was doing and came and stood next to me. I stared into his broad chest. Then he gripped my shoulders so I had to turn my eyes up to his face and meet his gaze. It was incredibly kind.

'It don't matter how you look, love. Those kids, they act funny maybe, but you've got to give 'em a chance. My youngest, Ben, he's Down's. He goes to school and he's got loads of mates. Don't give up on your life. All right?'

I felt the tears start to well, and hung my head so he wouldn't see. If Danny had been my dad then things would have been different. I would have been different.

'Look,' he said. 'It's a big world out there and this is a small place. Small town, small minds. You can be bigger than this. OK?' He patted me on my shoulder, kindly, with his big paw. I gave him a smile through the tears, scrubbing my face with the sleeve of my jumper. 'Now get back to those carrots!' I smiled again and peeled away.

The next day he invited me to go to his house for lunch, to meet his kids and his wife that Sunday.

'It's my day off. Cheryl does a great roast. Come over, she'd love to meet you.'

I didn't answer. It was my first invitation and what was I supposed to say? I wanted to thank him. But on Sundays I worked at home, there was the church to clean, the services to attend, the washing to do, the prayers to be said. The Mother would never let me off and, well, I wouldn't even try asking The Father. We hadn't spoken in over a week and it was better that way. So I just shook my head and he shrugged and tried not to look annoyed. I think I probably drive Danny mad, I bet he tells his wife I'm a wet fish, but I couldn't explain, I didn't have the words.

'Some other time, then. Let me know.'

I nodded and sloped off to make myself useful somewhere, sinking sands of disappointment clutching at my ankles. That night I lay in bed wondering how I might get to go to Danny's. Hephzi sniggers. If I couldn't even pluck up the guts to pay someone a friendly visit then how would I ever leave this place? I told her to be quiet and she says Danny's a stupid old bastard anyway. I decided I would have to risk it and lie.

Hephzi

Before

Friday I'm in knots, watching for Craig round every corner, in every class. He's nowhere and the disappointment makes me annoyed when Rebecca pesters me back at the vicarage that night.

'So you're really going to go to his party, then?'

'Yeah.'

I'm hanging out of the window gazing up at the sky. It's full of stars. The skies here stretch forever; I wonder where he is, under which little piece of heaven. I sigh.

'What if you get caught?'

I haven't told her what I said to Mother. I don't know why, it's just I need some secrets round here, and anyway I can't have Rebecca in my head one hundred per cent of the time. We used to tell each other everything but now things are different and she's going to have to get used to managing without me.

'Just cover for me, OK?'

I turn to look at her and she draws her knees up under her chin; her pyjamas are too short in the sleeves and legs, she's all elbows and ankles and that sad face. I sigh again and tut. She gets the message and crawls under her covers.

'It'll be fine, I promise. You're not going to get into any trouble and I'm going to have a great night. Be happy for me, Reb. OK?'

She shrugs from somewhere in the blankets and mutters something I don't hear. Who cares.

I can't sleep for worrying though.

About midnight it suddenly occurs to me that Craig might not really be into me after all. I don't exactly have much experience with these things, maybe I've read the signs all wrong, that could easily have happened. I'll look like a right idiot then. Or it could be a joke, I'll get there and they'll all point at me and laugh. I sit up in bed, horrified, and almost shake Rebecca awake to ask her what she thinks. But she's so still and peaceful for a change that I can't disturb her. Her nightmares usually keep her up half the night; I can sleep through them, thank goodness. Instead I send myself a message to remember to play it cool, not to seem too desperate and to let him do the chasing. Samara and Daisy laugh at girls who trail after guys – they're sad, losers, pathetic. I don't want people saying that about me. Like Samara said: treat 'em mean, keep 'em keen. It'll be hard though. I just want him to like me.

Even though I'm tired in the morning it doesn't matter. We clean and scrub the church steps and I hum as we go. Rebecca's eyes dart crossly in my direction, she can feel my anticipation and it's driving her crazy. I'm so excited I almost tell her to come too, then remember what Daisy said and bite my lip. I don't want people laughing at her. Or me. She wouldn't know what to wear, or say, or do, and she'd hang around me the whole time. She could look better if she tried a bit harder. She'll never be pretty or anything but really, once you're used to her, her face isn't that bad. Granny used to tell our parents they ought to take her to the doctors, the dentists, to hospital appointments for her hearing but they never did. Her hearing aids are old ones she got years ago when she had that fit after he hit her too hard and Mrs Sparks walked in so they had to take her to hospital. The nurses realized she couldn't hear and they fixed her up. Of course he charmed his way out of the whole business without much problem. People are so gullible, as soon as he tells them he's a vicar it's like he's said he's Jesus or something. In the end they fitted her out with that screw on her head and the little box which sits on it and for a while she said it was like people were shouting at her all day long. It soon got broken though, and she's back to mostly lip-reading now. If Mother snitches on me I'm going to tell about that too, about how they won't let my sister get her ears sorted or have her teeth done or go for surgery. I looked it up on the Internet and there are things they can do now to help people with her syndrome, things I didn't know about and I'm sure Rebecca has no idea of. When I'm free I'll help her, I won't leave her behind forever. Maybe she can even live with me and Craig, once he's used to her, and we can be a proper family.

It doesn't take me long to get ready. I have a bath, even though it's not allowed on a Saturday, or any day actually. But he's out so I can. He says a basin of cold water will suffice, the idiot. I wash my hair with the tiny bit of shampoo I have been storing up for this moment. It smells delicious. I love my hair and now it'll look and smell as gorgeous as it should. It's long, dark gold and wavy, even prettier than Daisy's. I pretend to be a mermaid and let it float around my face as I stretch out under the tepid water. Rebecca watches silently as I get dressed and dry my hair, then she comes over and sniffs.

'What's that?'

'Whaddya think, stupid?'

'Where'd you get it?'

'Samara's.'

'Did you steal it?'

'Just a bit.' I try not to let her annoy me. 'She wouldn't even notice, they had loads.' The last time I was round, I'd tipped as much as I could into a little plastic container I'd nicked from the science lab specifically for the purpose and I wasn't going to feel guilty. Why should other people have all the nice stuff? I reckon I deserve some too.

Rebecca goes quiet. She watches me.

'Is there any left?'

I stare at her and she blushes a deep tomato red. I nod slowly, 'Yeah, a bit, why?'

She shrugs and I root in my little bag and chuck the bottle over.

'Here. You can have it, all right?'

'Thanks.' She nods and shoves the bottle under her mattress. Treasure. Rebecca's hair's nice too, not as thick as mine but still pretty when it's clean and brushed. Hurrying to finish getting ready I put on the mascara, the blusher and lip gloss and turn for her assessment. She considers and then nods again.

'You look nice.'

'Oh, great, thanks a bunch.'

'Well, what do you want me to say?'

'Nothing. Forget it. I'm going now.'

'Are you just going to walk out of the front door? Like that's normal or something?'

'Yes. That is precisely what I am going to do, Rebecca. See ya!'

I dash out and down the stairs, the house is quiet and I'm pretty certain my parents still aren't in, they're probably next door in the church or visiting a parishioner. Which makes this my perfect opportunity. I hear my sister calling to me to be careful and pick up speed.

Craig's place isn't far but I'm calling for Samara first and so make a little detour. I'm walking so fast that I'm almost running and I stop myself from looking back into the shadows. I keep expecting a hand to appear out of the evening gloom, to clamp itself on my shoulder and propel me back to the vicarage where it will enact its revenge. It's no wonder I'm sweating by the time I get to Samara's.

She's ready and we try to dash straight off but her mum pulls us inside and gives us the third degree and makes Samara put a jumper on. But eventually we get away and run giggling down the road.

It's only half eight when we get to Craig's estate. I remind myself not to get drunk and puke this time, to be aloof and cool. I start forward for the house but Samara looks reluctant.

'It's too early.'

'Oh. Is it?'

'Yeah. No one gets to house parties this early.'

'What should we do, then?' I feel a bit silly all of a sudden.

'Daisy's going down the pub. Let's see if we can find her.'

I really don't want to do that and am just thinking how to talk her out of it when a group of lads pulls up in a car outside Craig's house. They pile out and up the drive, disappearing into the little house, which swallows them up whole.

'See?' I say, gesticulating, and we go closer, hearing the steady pump and pulse of music as we approach the house.

The front door's ajar, an open invitation, and we wend our way through the empty hall and front room into the kitchen. A couple of girls I don't recognize are pouring wine and laughing, they look us over then turn back to their conversation.

'Where's Craig?' I hiss at Samara.

'How should I know?' she hisses back and we stumble over the back step into the garden. Dark forms slowly morph into bodies as our eyes adjust again to the light, which is suddenly fading fast. The music's louder here and I feel a surge of blood to my heart and my mouth goes dry as someone moves out of the shadows, walking towards us.

'All right?'

I nod. Samara nods. Craig pauses and looks me up and down. He doesn't say anything. Then, 'D'you want a drink?'

'Yeah, please.' I've already forgotten that I'm supposed to be being careful, and can't wait for him to shove the cold bottle into my hand. The liquid tastes sweet and sharp and I take one swig then another. He hands me a cigarette too and, leaning close to light his own at the same time, the flame briefly illuminates his face and he smiles quickly into my eyes. Suddenly I'm having a good time.

More people arrive and I talk to girls I know from college and others I've never met before. Craig introduces me to his older brother Jamie and he gives me another bottle of sweet sticky alcohol and makes me laugh about something stupid. The music's louder and someone drags me to dance in the sitting room where disco lights are glimmering and glancing off the walls and all the furniture has been pushed to the sides of the room. I try to work out how the room really looks when it's just a normal day and wonder how come Craig's parents are letting him have this party. The thoughts don't stay in my head long enough to be more than tiny sparks firing into space and I dance with the others. Because it's dark it doesn't matter and I think I look as good as anyone else and work hard to copy the way they sway and move, mouthing words I don't know, grinning and swinging my hair, drinking from the endless supply of bottles which appear in my hand. What feels like hours later I realize I'm too hot and I struggle outside, hunting for air.

On the front lawn I spot Daisy. I've never seen the guy she's with before, he looks heaps older and has his arm tight round her shoulders, and hers just reaches round his waist. I lean against the wall of the house, feeling the rough brick press into my shoulders, and watch them for a while, waiting for the dizziness to settle. I don't want to feel drunk but I do and I wonder if I should sneak away now; I could make it home before I expose myself as an idiot in front of Craig. But if I do that I'll have lost my chance and there may not be another. Before Daisy can spot me I go back inside and upstairs to find a bathroom. If I hide out until I feel OK then maybe that would be all right, but the bathroom's locked and I need to find somewhere else to lie low. Going into what must be a bedroom I flick the switch and creep inside, feeling like a thief. It must be Craig's room, it's a bit of a tip and there's a guitar and amplifier in the corner, clothes strewn over the floor, a huge pile of books by the unmade bed. Guiltily I make my way over to the bed and sit down among the tumble of covers. The room smells different to our bedroom at home. It feels different too. Less like a cage, more like a den. My body tells me to lie down and so I do and I'm pretty sure I'm smiling as I fall asleep.

If Craig hadn't found me and woken me up God knows what would have happened. My head's banging and throbbing as I emerge from my sea of sleep and I immediately know I have to be sick. Pushing past him I dash for the bathroom and vomit. Tears come soon after and I perch on the side of the bath all shaky and ill. Someone knocks on the door and I know it's Craig when he speaks.

'Are you OK?'

I can't answer, there's nothing to say.

He tries again: 'Can I come in?'

I shake my head and rub my hands over my snotty, teary face; whatever make-up that had remained is now wiped in clownish stripes down my cheeks. Vomit rises and I remind myself I will never ever touch alcohol again. Craig comes in and I hide my face from him.

'Here.'

I hear the tap run and he's holding out a wet cloth. I take it and let it hang uselessly from my hands so he grabs it back and lifts my face up and wipes away the mess. My eyes are shut so I don't have to watch him pity me.

'There. You're all right now. How d'you feel?'

'A bit better, thanks.'

'Still feel sick?'

'No. I don't think so.'

'Good. You coming, then?'

He moves over to the door; I want to stop him, to keep him here, have him take care of me some more.

'Is the party over?' I ask at last.

'Nah, it's only one, still early, There's loads of people still here. Come down. I'll get you a drink.' He sees my face and laughs. 'Water, I mean.'

I manage to laugh too and he grabs my hand as we go back down the stairs and squeeze through the throng in the hallway and into the kitchen, which seems to have shrunk to half its original size. He shoulders people out of the way, pulling me with him, and eventually we find ourselves a corner by the sink. I'm firmly wedged into the space and Craig is between me and the rest of the world. He hands me a glass of water and I gulp it down.

'Better?'

I nod, this time meeting his eyes.

'Good.' He smiles at me, a real smile, and before I realize it he's moved his face next to mine and our lips are almost touching. He can't kiss me in the kitchen, I think, he can't, and he doesn't, instead he whispers in my ear.

'You look prettier without the make-up, you know.'

'Thanks a lot.'

He steps back and shrugs and now his smile has disappeared. I touch his sleeve.

'Can we go outside? I need some air.'

He pulls me through the crowds again, people try to stop him as we go but he keeps moving until we're in the back garden, where we began, hours ago. We perch on a couple of plastic chairs on the little paved patio. I stare out into the darkness, I sense Craig staring too.

I don't want him to abandon me but I can't think of a thing to talk about that will keep him there next to me. So I say the first thing that comes into my head.

'How come your parents let you have this party?'

'They don't know.'

'Oh my goodness, what are they going to do when they find out?'

'Dunno.'

'Aren't you worried about the place getting trashed?'

He shook his head. 'People round here know us. They wouldn't.'

I'm intrigued. 'What do you mean?'

He doesn't answer, gives his customary shrug.

'Do you really think I look horrible with make-up on?' I blurt out. Totally uncool.

'I didn't say that, did I?' He sighs. 'I just like girls when they look pretty, you know, natural. That was what I noticed about you first. You looked . . . fresh, different or something.'

How could I have looked fresh? Shut up in that vicar-age, day in, day out, we barely left the place unless it was on some miserable errand.

'Oh,' I say.

'Yeah, whatever, you do what you want though. People should always do what they want.'

'I agree. That's why I came tonight. My parents don't

know I sneaked out, but I wanted to come so I did.' I sound pathetic. I should never have started this conversation but sometimes I just want to tell someone everything.

'Why wouldn't they let you?'

He's looking at me more intently now as if he really wants to know and I know that I can't give him the real answer after all.

'Because I'm only sixteen. Because they've never met you. I dunno. It's just they're over-protective of us.' I play it down. 'You know what it's like, they think all kinds of stuff might happen.'

'Will you be in deep shit when you get back, then?'

'No, Rebecca, my sister, will cover for me.'

Damn, I hadn't meant to mention her but she's just slipped out, like she's been dying to make an appearance all evening.

'Your sister?'

'Yeah.'

He fishes his cigarettes out of his back pocket and offers me one. I shake my head.

'How come you aren't getting drunk?' I ask, watching him smoke.

'No point.'

'Don't you ever?'

'Nope. I smoke weed now and then but I can take it or leave it, the same with booze.'

Good, we can be sober together, I think.

'Are you really going to university? Daisy told me.'

'Maybe.'

'What will you study?'

'Medicine, I reckon. If I get in.'

'Why wouldn't you?'

'I don't reckon the teachers are going to give me good references, do you?'

'You'll have to start coming to college, then.'

He stares at me like I'm mad for a minute and then nods slowly. 'Maybe. My mum would love that.'

'Where is she?'

'Off with her boyfriend, some shitty little weekend away they had planned.'

'Don't you like her boyfriend, then?'

'Sharp, aren't you?'

I shut up, not liking his tone. Suddenly he's tense again and I edge uncomfortably on the chair and rub my arms, which are goose-pimpled in the night air.

'Here.' Craig is pulling off his sweatshirt and hands it to me. I pull it on, snuggling into what's left of his body heat and turn to thank him, but his face is right there and this time he really does kiss me. It's hot and cold all at once, his mouth tastes of cigarettes and something sweet, syrup or sugar. I kiss him back, like he's kissing me, and I don't want him ever to stop. We sit there like that, just kissing and not even talking, for ages. He puts his arms round me and pulls me close and I smile as his mouth covers mine again and again. But it can't last forever. *I have to go*, I tell myself, and eventually I pull away.

'I'd better get back.'

He nods and stands, pulling me to my feet. I wonder how I'll find my way in the dark and worry about what I might meet. I look at his watch, pulling his arm and pushing up his sleeve. Three a.m. *Please don't let me get caught now, please don't let this night be spoiled.* At the front of the house I pause, ready to say goodbye, but he carries on walking with me and we kiss and walk, kiss and walk all the way home. He doesn't want to talk much when we're not kissing and I don't mind, I'm just glad he's there. The vicarage rears up in front of us way too soon. I pull him to a stop and whisper goodbye.

'I can't come in, then?' He pulls a mock disappointed face and I give him a play frown.

'See you on Monday,' I say instead. 'Please come to college.'

He nods. 'OK. For you.'

Then I sprint away, up the path and round the back, in and up the stairs and collapse into my bed. The whole house is silent, my breathing sounds like an invading army and I'm sure I must have woken someone somewhere. The room reverberates with the thudding of my heart, I can hear it boom and I huddle under the covers trying to silence the racket. But I'm smiling like a crazy girl. I'll never stop smiling again.

Rebecca

After

It took me another week to really believe I could do it. I wasn't sure I'd be safe, going all that way; I was sure to get lost and no one would help me and then I'd never find my way back. The world was a sea of danger and I could easily drown out there.

Rubbish. You talk a whole load of rubbish, Rebecca. You'll be safer out there than here!

Maybe Hephzi was right.

Sunday arrived. I crept into the bathroom and washed carefully then put on Hephzi's blue jumper. It was a find; Hephzibah had fished it out of one of the charity bags before they'd been sent away. It was brand new when she discovered it and it went well with my eyes.

'Mother. I have to work today.'

She snapped her head round to stare at me. I was standing by the kitchen door, she was making a pot of tea. It would be weak; the teabags were always used at least twice before they were ever thrown away. For a moment the sun caught her face and I could almost see through her skin to the bones and blood beneath, running as thinly as the brew she stirred.

'No. You have your chores here.'

'Well, I'm afraid they need me at the home. I already said I'd go in. One of the other carers has come down with a bug. You'll have to manage without me for a change.'

'I won't get the church ready without you.' She checked her watch. Wisps of panic spiralled from under her dressing-gown and she began to hurry, hot tea spurting from the teapot as she muttered incomprehensible words beneath her breath. The Father would be waiting for his breakfast upstairs, as he preferred. To keep her calm, I gave in a little.

'I'll make a start. But I'll be off before the first service.'

She nodded and scurried up to him. I wondered what she would say and waited for the holler, the retribution. If I heard him coming then I decided I'd run for it, straight out of the back door like a sparrow evading a hawk. The Mother's handbag was on the side and I could grab that and make a clean break. But there were no unusual sounds. Somehow I'd got away with it.

The church was cold and I started with the polishing. Everything was still clean from yesterday but he would notice the slightest speck of dust, the faintest smudge or print. Inside I buzzed. I was going to Danny's because he'd invited me. I was going to Danny's because he was my friend. I was going to Danny's because I said so, *I* said so.

Euphoria made everything so much easier, so much faster. If I could do this then maybe I could do anything. The place was almost ready by nine o'clock and as my mother came in I nodded to her and grinned. For once I didn't hide my mouth but let the smile spill over her as it split my face in two. Her shock spurred me faster home for my bag. I had saved enough for the bus fare there and back; Danny lived nearer town than us and it was much too far to walk.

I suppose they weren't expecting me so early. It was only half past ten by the time I got off the bus, but it took me a while to wander around and find the house. Everywhere felt unfamiliar. We've always stayed in the village, apart from obligatory church events and The Father's forays to far-flung towns with unfamiliar names, so my sense of direction was woeful. Every road and house looked the same to me, neat rows of identical boxes lined up and watching me with impassive eyes. I tried to think carefully about Danny's directions. I'd listened with all my might as he'd told me the way, just in case I changed my mind, he'd said. Hephzi is cross and won't come. She thinks if I'm going to break out then I could at least do something fun, not go hanging round some old bloke who reeks of cooking, to waste the day with his boring, retard family. Now was not the time for an argument though, so I ignored her, she has to let me take my time. If I want to I can switch her off, although I know she'll scream at me later for being mean. She wasn't all that happy about lending me her blue jumper either but that's tough. Everything of mine is horrid and I wanted to look nice. Nicer than usual anyway.

So it was only eleven o'clock when I pressed what I'd worked out had to be the right bell. I'd walked up and down the path three times before deciding for sure. My breath juddered and suddenly I regretted coming. What if he hadn't meant it? What if I'd got the wrong house? That would be just like me to read the whole thing wrong. Maybe that's what normal people did, maybe they invited each other round all the time but didn't really mean it, perhaps it was one of those 'normal' things Hephzi and I were never too sure about. A dark shape appeared behind the door, fiddling with the locks, and then it was too late to run. A woman pulled the door open. Dressed in jeans and a pink T-shirt, she looked at me curiously. Then her face fell. I noticed the change before she could swiftly lift the corners of her mouth into a fake, hard smile.

'Hello? Can I help you?'

She thought I was there to bother her. Maybe selling something. Tea towels, lucky heather or, perhaps, God. Danny hadn't told her I was coming. I looked down and mumbled why I was there.

'Sorry?'

'Danny invited me. I'm sorry, I shouldn't have come . . .' There was a pause. It was impossible to tell what she was thinking.

'Hang on a minute, love. You're not the girl from the care home, are you?'

I nodded and she pulled the door wider and gesticulated

that I should go inside, but I hesitated, not sure now. If only Danny were here, he'd make this better.

'Is Danny here?'

'No, he's taken the kids to football. Well, Archie and Mac. Ben's in the front room and Milly's upstairs. You're all right, love, you can come in. I'm Cheryl, Danny's wife.'

I stayed hovering on the step. They weren't expecting me. I was going to be in the way, a nuisance, and a minute ago she'd looked at me like she wanted to vomit.

I almost turned round but then someone grabbed me and started to tug; an insistent little hand latched on to mine and I looked down at the boy who was dragging me forward, crowing hello, and before I could run I was inside, standing on the clean laminate floor, wondering what on earth to do next.

'Trust Danny not to let me know we were going to have a visitor!' Her voice was falsely bright like a plastic flower and I sensed the annoyance she was trying to cover up. 'You go on and sit down and wait in the living room with Ben. Danny won't be long.'

What about lunch? I thought. Danny had said there'd be lunch. I couldn't smell anything cooking and it had gone eleven. Maybe she'd be starting it now; I wondered if I should offer to help. But then Ben dragged me into the living room and I slid on to the leather sofa. Ben stared at me.

'Hi,' I mumbled. 'I'm Rebecca.'

He smiled at me and for a second I relaxed but then he

reached up and touched my face. I jerked away from the little hand like I'd been scalded and he whimpered and looked sad.

'Sorry, Ben,' I whispered. He shook his head, his lower lip thrusting forward. I hoped he wouldn't cry. If he cried I decided I would have to make a run for it, his mum would think I'd hurt him or something. Oh God, it was all going wrong.

I told you this was a waste of time. You might just as well have stayed at the vicarage with them. Utterly pathetic.

Shut up. I thought you weren't coming, I hissed back at Hephzi and took a deep breath as Cheryl appeared at the door.

'You want a cup of tea? Coffee?' She was smiling, her hands on her hips, and waiting for a normal answer to a normal question. Ben skittered off to hang on to his mum's legs. Absently she caressed his head.

'No, thank you. Can I help at all?'

'What with?'

'Oh. Anything. I'm good at veg.'

'Veg?' She pursed her lips and stared at me, then realized what I'd meant. 'Bloody hell! He didn't invite you round for your dinner, did he?'

Before I could deny it the front door opened and the hall was full of voices. Now I was trapped. I could hear Hephzi laughing from somewhere far away. I wished she'd shut up. Cheryl marched into the hall. I strained to hear what she was going to say about me.

'You've got a visitor.'

'Oh yeah?'

Danny came in, red-cheeked and wearing tracksuit bottoms and a T-shirt. He did a double take then grinned at me.

'You came! Brilliant!'

I searched his voice for signs of sarcasm, anger, resentment. There was none. Behind him Cheryl was smiling at me again. Perhaps I'd read her wrong. I'm not good at understanding people.

'You might have warned me, Dan. I was only going to do leftovers. We're going to your mum's for dinner, remember?'

'Oh yeah. Doesn't matter, does it, Rebecca? You don't mind, do you?'

He came over to me and hooked an arm round my shoulders and squeezed me to him tightly. His bulk and warmth made me feel like I was being swaddled and I let myself sag against him for a second.

Cheryl rolled her eyes. 'Typical!' she said, laughing, and I couldn't help the grin, it opened my mouth and spread my cheeks wide without my permission. Quickly I covered my mouth with my hand. Then Danny laughed.

'Great, that's more like it. I'll call the lads, introduce you.'

His sons had disappeared into the garden to carry on kicking their football around and Ben had run after them and was getting in the way. They didn't mind and passed the ball to him, cheering when he kicked in the right direction. I watched them through the French windows; it was safer behind the glass.

It was probably one of the best days of my life. We ate pizza for lunch then huge slices of chocolate gateau, all from the freezer, Cheryl said, but to me it was manna from heaven. Then we played on the Wii. Archie taught me how to do it, putting his hand over mine and showing me how to move the controls – it turned out I was quite good at downhill skiing. No one looked at me like I was a freak, no one threw stuff at me like they used to in Maths, and Ben even came and sat on my knee and gave me a hug. I wanted to talk more, to explain who I was, but I didn't think my words would have been right so I kept quiet. It didn't seem to matter, no one stared. Milly even did my nails with her pearly pink varnish that she'd got free with a magazine. She's only twelve but looks older than me. At half past five it was time for them to go off visiting, which meant I had to go too. I wished I could go along with them but I didn't dare ask. In the hall, getting ready to leave, I caught Archie's eye. I'd decided already he was cute, small for sixteen with a cheeky grin.

'So, what is it that's wrong with you, then?' Immediately I flushed and looked down. Of course they'd noticed, I chastised myself. I'd been kidding myself that I was just the same and could be one of them. When I didn't answer he spoke again and I could tell he was feeling bad.

'Sorry . . . I wasn't being, you know . . .' The words hung

in the air, little bullets he never meant to fire. I drew a
deep breath then got it all out in a rush.

'It's a syndrome.'

'Like Down's?'

'No. Well a bit. It's called Treacher Collins. But apart
from my face there's nothing wrong with me. I'm normal
apart from that.' Normal. Me, normal. I hadn't known I
was going to say that but now that I had I realized it could
be true. The words had come out in a rush, totally
unplanned and uncensored, and it hit me that I'd just
made it sound like I thought his brother Ben was a freak.
But he nodded as if he understood what I meant.

'Are you at college, then?'

'No, I had to leave.'

'Why?'

I shrugged, still keeping my eyes on the floor. I had
never spoken with a boy like this before, apart from the
time I'd met up with Craig at the Rec and I'd been trying
to forget that that had ever happened.

'Didn't you like it?'

He was trying to talk to me again and I shook my head,
hardly holding up my end of the conversation. *Pathetic*,
Hephzi mutters in my ear. Cheryl interrupted us before I
could try again.

'Come on then, you two. We'd best get off. See you,
love, it was nice to meet you. Danny's not stopped talking
about you, you know!' She gave me a brief hug and I
flushed in pleasure and stuttered out a thanks. I watched

on the drive as they pulled off in their people carrier. Archie waved from the back, smiled and mouthed something, I couldn't make out what, and I wondered what it might have been as I walked back to the bus stop. The sun seemed to hang lower now in the early summer sky and I moved to catch its rays, still wanting to feel warm. They'd have given me a lift, but once they were all in there wasn't any room for extras.

On the journey home I felt the glow of the day fade as if someone were brushing me down and restoring me to my dull, everyday self. It didn't matter now that Cheryl had hugged me and Ben had sat on my knee and Archie had asked me what I thought about college. I realized I was hungry again. Perhaps there would be something to eat when I got back, even if it was one of The Mother's roasts. *Fatty*, says Hephzi and I laugh. If there's one thing I'm not, it's fat. Hephzi was curvier than me, she had breasts and hips and a bum even, though she was super slim. Men looked at her when she walked past. Not me, I'm straight up and down. I knew there was no point thinking about Archie, he wouldn't look twice at me. *Or once*, says Hephzi. I told her to shut up. She doesn't need to remind me of what I am.

The bus had taken forever, going all around the houses, and I felt the day begin to narrow as the passengers disembarked. The closer we came to the village, the darker and smaller everything seemed. It was late when I finally reached the vicarage. I walked slowly towards the door.

The whole place looked as though it were already shut up for the night, and my feet dawdled as I came up the garden path. It hit me that he'd be waiting, ready to dole out a measure of pain, just so much as befitted the crime, if not a little extra to make sure I'd been taught the lesson. I wondered what I should do. I didn't want to go in yet, not if he was waiting right behind the door, so I scooted down the side of the house to Hephzi's tree. The last time I'd tried climbing up was when we'd been seven or eight and I'd fallen and banged my head and twisted my ankle. Hephzi had kissed it better. *Yuck*, she says, *I wouldn't do that now*. But at least she said she would show me the best footholds and how to place my hands, even though she kept moaning about how ridiculous it was to return to the vicarage at all. I'd made all that effort, why was I going back?

I stared up through the thick canopy of leaves and branches and beyond into little patches of twilight, considering. Granny had read a book to us when we were really little and I remembered it then, a story about some children who climbed a tree and found a new world waiting for them every time they reached the top; maybe The Land of Goodies, or, if you were really lucky, The Land of Do-As-You-Please. Hephzi and I had listened, enraptured, as Granny had read aloud and I'd dreamed of the slippery-slip and sliding out of our room and into a world as free as that dream.

Hephzi was getting fed up now. She doesn't like the

cold and it was beginning to get chilly. She thinks the whole idea sucks.

I faced facts. I didn't want to go in. I'd been free for a day and it had been wonderful. I liked Danny and Cheryl and Archie and the other kids. They were so kind and nice and all just got on with each other, even if they did argue over the remote control or squabble over the next game they would play. The kids talked to their mum and dad in normal voices, no one sounded like they were choking or shrank back from an outstretched hand. I realized that this was what Hephzi had wanted for herself and that it was this that she'd hoped to find at Craig's. She hadn't been looking for just a boyfriend, she'd wanted the whole thing. The normal house and the normal parents. The nice bedroom and fluffy towels, a pile of magazines and nail varnish to try out. She'd wanted to watch TV and slump about like a normal teenager. When I'd told her not to rely on Craig I hadn't really understood. Now it was all clear.

I could walk away, back down the path. If I didn't go back into the vicarage then I wouldn't have to see the wall. I wouldn't have to hear the babies' cries.

The spare bed in the home was free. Suki and Michaela were on night duty and they hurried to let me in when they spotted me at the back door and fed me hot chocolate and digestive biscuits, smiling through their puzzlement as I explained that I'd lost my key and that my parents were out. Eventually I think they got the message, because they didn't protest when I trundled down the corridor to the nurse's bed, kicked off my shoes and dived in. As I nodded off I knew I was going to have the best night's sleep ever. I'd made it out of the vicarage for the first night in years and no one could disturb me here. *See?* I told Hephzi, *I can be normal too.* She didn't answer.

Morning came so quickly. There had been no hovering ghoul at my shoulder crying for food, demanding a lullaby or whispering nightmares into my dreams and so I was full of energy and enjoyed my breakfast, starting work straight afterwards, even finding time to sit with Cyrilla and read her fifty pages or so of a historical novel we hadn't tried. In the end she nodded off and I curled up in the chair and finished the book. I knew at some point I'd have to go back to the vicarage but I was enjoying fantasising that I could live in the home forever. I had friends here.

Danny came in at lunchtime, taking over for the afternoon shift. I'm not sure if he noticed that I was wearing the same clothes as I'd had on the day before, it's not actually that unusual and under my tabard you couldn't really tell. But he did ask if I'd got back OK and I turned away to lie.

'You'll have to come for a barbie next time. Summer's more or less here.'

I nodded, yes, brilliant. If I'd broken out once, then I could do it again. At last I understood Hephzi's intoxication with freedom and I wanted another shot, to feel the swell of happiness in my veins until it exploded like tiny fireworks in my brain. Danny didn't mention Archie and I tried not to mind, I hadn't really been expecting him to. Then, just as I was going, he called me back.

'I forgot to say. Archie's having some trouble with his homework. He needs his English GCSE to get into college next year –' Danny looked annoyed about this – 'but he's not much cop. None of us is. I can't spell for toffee. Anyway, I've seen you with them books. How about it?'

'What?'

'Helping him out a bit.'

'Oh. I don't know. How?'

'Just give him a few pointers. He says the teacher's useless and he's got this coursework. Some Shakespeare malarkey.'

'I've never read any Shakespeare.'

For a moment he looked crestfallen but he brightened up fast. 'Well. You'll soon get the hang of it. Can't be hard for a bright cookie like you. Shall I tell him you're up for it?'

'All right.'

My hands were shaking when I left as the excitement took hold. I was a bright cookie. He thought I could help Archie. Well, I would try. I was so preoccupied with the thought of it that I didn't notice my legs carrying me up the driveway to the vicarage and round to the back door. The Mother was in the kitchen, I could see her at the stove, her shoulders hunched and thin under her thick wool sweater. She had to be boiling in that; it was the hottest day of the year so far. I pushed open the door and went inside. The room smelled rancid. The Father would not be pleased if she'd forgotten to wash. The Mother had been getting like that more and more since Hephzi had died and he had to tell her all the time to scrub up, to tidy her hair, to smile more sweetly. But you can't hide poison forever, it has to seep out sometime and I could smell it on the air. I couldn't wait to get out of the room and fly upstairs and sit and plan how I'd help Archie. She swung around, her wooden spoon held up like a weapon, her face only growing grimmer when she saw it was me.

'Hi.' I wondered what she'd do if I smiled at her again.

'Where've you been? You've been gone all night.' Her voice was as rough as sandpaper, scratching at me, scraping for a row.

'At work. I stayed at the home. Ask if you don't believe me.'

She shook her head, her mouth a narrow line.

'He should never have agreed to it. He's always been too soft, letting you and Hephzibah run rings around us.'

'What are you talking about?'

'That job. It's time you called it a day. I can't have you swanning off like that for days at a time, there's work to do here. You can stay at home.'

'I don't want to.'

Yes, whispers Hephzi. *Tell her, tell her again!*

She advanced towards me, brandishing the spoon. Up close I saw the bags under her eyes and the broken veins on her cheeks dancing over her face in a bloody web. She looked old, and I stepped backwards. Her pale, blank eyes sought mine.

'You're getting just like her, just like the other one. She came and went as she pleased and now you think you can do the same. And you'll go the same way, mark my words, you'll go the same way.'

Retreating further and skirting round the kitchen table to the door, I ran from her, although her hectoring followed me up the stairs.

'You don't know how lucky you are!' she called to my retreating back and I stumbled, startled all over again by this woman who called herself my mother. I knew she wouldn't chase me, she was all talk without him to back her up and her words weren't going to hurt me now. Instead I reminded myself that I'd got away with it all, so far, and that there were better things to come.

I'd need to be clever though and take things one step at a time.

No! shouts Hephzi. *No!* But I ignored her again.

I sat at the window, avoiding the wall, and thought about The Parents. The last thing they'd ever want would be for people to realize how sick and twisted they were. So I had to exploit that. I thought of Mrs Sparks, round here every other day or so, the vicar's right-hand woman, or so she'd like to think. I'd never liked her, simply on principle, but reflecting now I could see she'd never been anything but kind to Hephzi and me. Sometimes she'd brought round bags of clothes, things her own daughters had grown out of, colouring pens when we were little, or a box of books. We never saw most of it but Hephzi usually managed to swipe a few nice bits from the clothes bags before The Mother whisked the unsuitable booty away. And I had Mrs Sparks to thank for my job. She'd suggested it and he had been unable to refuse her without making himself subject to talk. Talk meant gossip and gossip is the devil's radio. I suppose he thought, what with the care home being right next door, it'd be easy to keep me under surveillance. Well, that's what he thought. Hephzi was watching me and sneering.

Smug, are we? she says. *You reckon you got away with that yesterday?*

I shrugged, it was obvious she was annoyed and I didn't want to provoke her.

Just you wait, they'll get you back. She pauses, goading me. *Unless you get out first, that is. What did you come back for anyway, idiot? You were free!*

I didn't want to listen right then so I crawled under the bed and closed my eyes, thinking about Archie and Shakespeare.

Hephzi

Before

I'm expecting to see Craig at school on Monday, just like he promised, but he doesn't show. It's the same on Tuesday and Wednesday. Slowly the drug of Saturday night wears off and I'm left feeling empty, like I just failed some test I didn't even know I'd been taking. Maybe I made the whole thing up, maybe I fantasized the entire night. When he doesn't even send me a message on Facebook to say hi or to explain I start to wonder what I've done to make him hate me. I catch Daisy looking my way in the common room and I know she's desperate to ask me what happened but I'm not telling anyone. Not now.

On Thursday, when I've given up hope and am slouching to class with Rebecca, someone grabs me from behind, circling my waist and whizzing me up into the air. I squeal in surprise and Rebecca shouts something incomprehensible. Then I hear him laughing and realize it's Craig at last, holding me tight, there in the corridor, like that's totally normal in-character behaviour for him. I laugh too and let him kiss me right on the mouth in front of everyone.

'Where've you been?' I eventually manage to say. He

shrugs, just like you'd expect, but there is happiness dancing in his eyes and a smile is twitching his lips. Rebecca
tries to pull me away and along to our lesson. He looks at
her curiously, like he's never noticed her before, and all
three of us arrive at Maths just about on time. Craig's
presence is a boon for the teacher, who goes to town on
the sarcastic welcome. He picks on him for the whole lesson but Craig answers nearly every question right and
helps me with my work. He's some kind of living calcula-
tor or something, swinging in his chair, spewing out
answers like he doesn't even have to try. I never realized
how sexy a guy with brains could be.

The bell goes and he grabs my hand and drags me
behind him out of the class and out of the building.
Behind the gym he kisses me like he's just had forty days
in the desert and I'm a glass of water. Pushing him away
at last I catch my breath. I've never seen Craig look so
happy, it's like he's a different person.

'You look different.'

He raises an eyebrow. A new trick, maybe an improve-
ment on the shrugging.

'You look hot.' His tone is accusatory and I can't keep
my cool. I go bright pink. He kisses me again, mumbling
into my hair.

'Especially when you blush.'

'So, what now?'

He stares at me, pushing the hair back from my face,
drinking me in. I fidget and squirm.

'I reckon we get out of here. What do you think?'

I nod and we race off the premises before anyone can stop us. My bag bangs against my legs as I run, holding his hand, a few steps behind, but it doesn't matter, nothing matters now.

We spend the day back at his place, in his room, listening to music. He tells me about the trouble he was in because of the party, the fight with his mum's boyfriend, and that he's been staying at his brother's flat in town for the past few days until things calmed down.

'Sorry I let you down. I wanted to see you but, well, I had to keep out of the way.'

I can understand this and nod. Then he plays me a song he's written and I ask what it's about.

'Can't you guess?' he looks at me, teasing, smiling, flirting again and the blush is back. I sense that I really shouldn't be here on my own in his bedroom in the middle of a school day. Anything could happen and Rebecca will be going spare.

'It's about you, of course.'

He puts his guitar down and wraps his arms around me. By the time he's finished kissing me it's almost dark outside.

'I'd better go home.'

'Stay.'

'I can't!'

He groans. 'All right. I'll walk you.'

On the way he tells me that he's taking his bike test next

week and that he's saved up enough to buy a second-hand moped his brother's mate's selling. He'll take me away then, he says, we'll go to the seaside for fish and chips and ice cream, he'll take me up to London and show me all the sights. He can't believe it when I say I've never been and he wants to know why not. But we're home and I run inside before he can kiss me goodbye or ask any more awkward questions.

They're all sitting there at the supper table. I can hear the house creaking and whining in the dead silence. No one is eating and the food looks as if it's been congealing on the plates for days. I check my watch and realize I'm over an hour late for dinner. Silently I slide into my place and I feel Rebecca's shoe meet my ankle, a gentle, insistent pressure, warning me to watch out. Father picks up his fork and takes a mouthful of his dinner. Then, in an explosion of shattering glass and china, the plates are smashed on the floor, the food is hanging from the walls, he's screaming and shouting at me and Rebecca and Mother. I push Rebecca behind me and suddenly, for the first time, I'm not afraid.

'What the hell's wrong with you?' I scream at him, into his face, although he doesn't hear me above the sound of his own rage. He reaches for my neck, swaying in his alcohol-induced frenzy, but I duck and we scarper fast.

Barricaded in our room, under Rebecca's bed, which is wedged against the door, all I can hear is the ragged edges of our breathing. Downstairs, the smashing and banging and swearing continues and I hope Mrs Sparks pops in to witness St Roderick's freak-out.

'Why did you have to do it?' Rebecca whispers eventually. 'Why couldn't you just come home on time? He's going to kill us now.'

'No, he isn't. Don't worry.'

Rebecca half grunts, half sobs. She's sharp with anger and fear and I know it's partly because I've been with Craig.

'Listen, Reb, don't be cross with me, you mustn't. I'm happy!'

'Well, bloody good for you!' she explodes and lashes out at me with her fists and legs, flailing at me, her elbows jabbing my flesh in the cramped space. I grab her and stop her easily and she weeps into the carpet.

'You're going to leave me here with him, aren't you? You're going to go off with that horrible boy and leave me here and I'll never escape. I hate you, Hephzi, I hate you.'

'Stop it, Reb,' I whisper into her shoulder. 'Stop it. I love you. I love you.'

We lie there tangled in the dark space under the bed because it feels safer than venturing up. Sometimes my sister cries and screams in her sleep but I don't dare ask her what her nightmares are about; I don't think she'd tell me anyway. While Rebecca mumbles and moans beside me I wonder what I'm going to say to Craig about everything here. Some things are pretty hard to keep secret and I don't want to have to start lying to him. But I'll have to,

I can't see another way. If he knew, he'd look at me differently and he'd know I wasn't right.

October is our month. I sneak off from college almost every day. Craig passes his test, like he said he would, and we ride the bike as far as we can, sometimes just out into the fens, maybe to the water meadows or into town to meander through the shops. He points out stuff he'll buy me when he's rich and I smile and picture it so easily. Our future glows like a sun in my imagination. When I'm sitting behind him, holding on for dear life as he drives fast enough to catch the speed of light, I think we might take off. Fly away and be free. I dream of it, sick and scared and ready for anything, just so long as I can keep my arms around Craig. No one else matters any more. I see Daisy in the corridors and smile and wave and don't care what she might be saying about me. Funnily enough, she's always in my face now Craig and I are an item, inviting me out, lending me stuff, giving me things, passing me notes. Because I'm so happy I forget what she said about my sister and let her be my friend. On the days I'm in college Craig is too and the others latch on to him, he's like a magnet, he just sits there and they come, and I sit and smile and watch, proud.

Daisy doesn't really like it. Samara says she's jealous even though she's got a boyfriend of her own. I don't care that she's angry, not now I've got Craig, but when we're at school she's either my best friend or making my life a misery.

Craig and I are eating lunch in the common room, two weeks after we began going out, when she starts. Craig's got me a sandwich and a can of Coke; I've no idea what Rebecca's having, but she'll have lost herself in a book and forgotten all about food. Anyhow, I see Daisy looking at me, thinking, a bit like a snake watching a mouse, and I wait for what she'll say this time.

'D'you know what, Hephzi? I reckon I know your dad.' Her voice is super-sly.

I swallow a mouthful and I don't look up. Maybe if I ignore her she'll leave it.

'He used to run that Saturday club, didn't he, every weekend, even in the holidays? My mum used to make me go – free childcare, she said. We were remembering it last night, when we were talking about you. She feels really bad about it now.'

I know she wants me to ask what she's been saying about me; she likes that, Daisy does, tantalizing you, making you hang off her every word. But I remember easily enough what she's talking about. One of Roderick's recruitment drives. He let me go too: me and Mrs Sparks and Mother and a couple of others were his 'team', he said. It was fun, one of the best things I got to do as a kid. We weren't allowed to do any of the normal things, not even go to school, and I'd always longed to go to the primary, to wander round the classrooms and just be with the other children. We'd peer through the school railings as we walked past, trailing behind our mother, our heads turning to catch an extra glance as we went by. We'd see the pastel walls and the children's paintings, the pictures and bright smiling faces; the hustle and bustle and all those colours and shapes jumped out at us from behind the big windows and tempted me to reach out and touch. I imagined having my own poem or collage up there on a wall and how proud I'd be. I'd draw a picture of a garden and two little girls. Me and Reb. Sometimes we'd see the kids out in the playground, running and shrieking or swinging upside down on the climbing frames, maybe hopscotching with their friends. I tried to jump like they did, but on the pavement squares. It wasn't the same.

Daisy's voice cuts in. 'Yeah, d'you still do that, then? Help out Daddy with his Jesus army?'

I meet her eye at last. Her head is tipped to one side and a tricky smile is playing on her lips. Daisy could never even dream the truth. I shrug and answer slowly.

'I never went to the Saturday school, that's his church stuff. I do my own thing.'

'Bollocks, I remember you. You were the one handing out the name tags.'

She's right. I remember standing there with Roderick's hands tight on my shoulders as I peeled off the stickers and he grinned hello at each and every one of them, how I solemnly handed the tag to each newcomer, wondering if maybe this one, or maybe that one, might be my friend.

'Well, maybe I went a couple of times. Big deal.'

Craig looks from me to her and back to me. Then he

concentrates on his lunch again, not interested.

'They taught us all those stupid songs, those actions. God, it was so embarrassing! I can't believe I let my mum make me go there.'

It comes back, booming through the speakers of the past, Dad on the makeshift stage he'd rigged up in the church hall, shouting Bible verses down a crackling microphone, his arms in the air, pouring his excitement into their ears as he strutted back and forth, whipping the children up, encouraging them to join him. Some of the grown-ups, who were also church helpers, participated in his frenzy; they looked as if someone had lit them up from within as they reached out their hands in praise, an orgy of oblation. I put down my food, hardly hungry now.

'He's a nutter, your dad, isn't he? That's what my dad says anyway, one of those religious nutters.'

'Yeah, whatever,' I say and pick up my bag. She smirks, happy she's twisted a knife somewhere and made me feel different.

The Saturday club hadn't mortified me at the time. I'd felt special to be chosen to go, they didn't let Rebecca. Now though I don't want to think about it, how he'd build himself up each week as if he were out to conquer the world, all dressed up in his special trendy jeans and Mr Men T-shirt. 'Mr Happy' it said on the front underneath the round, smiling yellow figure. I'd watch the way he held the little kids' hands, how he hugged them tight, whispering into their ears that Jesus loved them and that they should come to Jesus. I'd been about ten or eleven when I'd been allowed to join the team, just so excited to be meeting other children at last. He gave it up eventually. The effort outweighed the gain. We rarely saw those kids at the services on Sundays but I kept looking out for them even so. Granny had wasted her time when she'd tried to persuade Mother to let us go to school.

'Why don't you let them go, love? Give yourself some time off from all this home-schooling? They'd love it, meeting all the other little kiddies, all the fresh air and fun.'

'The children are fine here. It's out of the question.'

'Why, though? I don't understand.'

And Granny didn't get it. She never understood them and they got sick of her trying to interfere.

'I'll have a word with Roderick, shall I? Tell him what I think?'

'No,' Mother hissed at her. 'Just leave it, would you?'

Granny did keep trying though, right to the end, I'm sure she did.

For some reason Rebecca still hates Craig. I've explained to her a million times why I like him and she's seen for herself in class how clever he is. I tell her how he plays the guitar and writes songs for me, I even show her some of his lyrics, sure that will convince her, but she just sneers and turns her back on me. I know she's jealous, I just don't know what to do about it. I don't know why I even care.

But it's not all easy. After the first night, the night at Craig's party when everything started, Mother grabbed me in the quiet of the church as I polished the lectern, shaking me out of my happiness. She circled my wrist with her bony fingers and told me she wouldn't cover up for me again, do or say what I might, she wasn't putting herself at risk one more time. I begged, I threatened, I cried, but it made no difference. And so all I asked was that she kept her mouth shut. And that's when I found the tree.

There's no way I'm going to give up my freedom and stay locked up in the vicarage when I could be with Craig. So I've devised my own escape route and I'm pretty proud of it. It means that I can sneak out and see Craig as often as I like, so long as Roderick's dead drunk or out on some visit or just plain old asleep. I love my tree; even though I've got scrapes and scratches down my arms and up my legs, it doesn't matter one bit. Craig thinks I'm mad. I've tried to explain to him that my parents are strict and insist he always gets me home on time, but he reckons that if I give them a chance they'll get used to him and I won't have to sneak around any more. I let him have his fantasy and keep the truth to myself.

He's introduced me to his mum though. At first I didn't know what to say or where to look. I don't know many normal mums, so I settled for smiling a lot and agreeing with whatever she said. She's dead nice. She keeps inviting me round for tea but I never can say yes. If she's home during the day when I'm there I sit at their kitchen table with her and we chat about any old thing. Craig says she keeps threatening to come to one of Father's services and to make him go too. She thinks it's important that she at least introduces herself. I told him over my dead body and he agreed, so I hope he keeps her away. If she were to show up and talk to him then everything would be over.

I'm surprised I can sleep at night these days, there are so many things to worry about, so many ways in which I could be found out. Rebecca never stops reminding me either, like some tragic soothsayer she drones on and on about the risk and the danger. I can't bear it, sometimes I want to sew up her mouth or cover her head with my pillow until she shuts up all together.

Pam, that's Craig's mum, is painting her house and she's given me what she's got left over from doing the living room. I smuggle it home, and a spare brush, and start straight in on the wall by my bed. Our room hasn't been painted or papered for as long as I can remember. The wallpaper is faded now but you can almost make out a pattern of flowers, blooming here and there; it must have been pretty once. Maybe the family here before us cared enough to make the room nice. I paint until my arm aches and I have to take a break. I don't really know why I'm bothering, it won't be long until I'm out of here, I hope, if things go to plan. Sighing, I survey my handiwork and realize that I need to go over it all again. I'll never have the money to buy more but maybe Pam will have a bit extra going spare. When I've got my own house and my own family I'm going to paint the rooms all the colours of the rainbow, just like Pam is. She wants to do Craig's room orange but he won't let her and says he wants it left alone. When they argue it's not like when I fight with my mother and father – no one explodes, no one disintegrates, they just bicker, slam a door and forget it.

Our father has a book. In it he lists everything we do that, according to him, is wrong, and sometimes he'll get it out and read it through, adding and amending as he goes. We have to kneel and listen; it's one of his rituals, and I'm pretty sick of it. I won't let him touch me now, no more hair brushing, no more hand holding, no more hitting. He's getting madder and stranger and soon he'll lose it, there's only so far even I can push him and I'm right at the limits. I've got to get out of here.

'What are you doing?'

'What's it look like?'

'Why are you painting that wall, I mean?'

I don't answer Rebecca, sometimes her questions are just too damn stupid to even bother with.

'Are you going out again tonight?'

I nod.

'When will you be back?'

'Who knows? He's at a meeting, you know, the school-board thing. It'll be safe, don't worry.'

She always worries, no matter what I say, and it makes

me nervous too. But I have to go tonight, it's special, it's Craig's birthday. His eighteenth. He should be in the year above us but he missed so many lessons when he was younger they wouldn't let him move up when he should have been going into Year Ten, they said he was too far behind. It's stupid, when he's the cleverest person I know. But teachers like doing stuff like that, they like to make a point, just for the sake of it. Year Nine was when Craig's dad left, but no one bothered to find that out. When Craig was bunking off he was out looking for his dad, he told me, but he never did manage to find him. He just disappeared into thin air. I managed not to say lucky you, but that's what I was thinking. I told Rebecca about it and she went quiet for a very long time.

'Do you think that might happen to us? Do you think one day he'll just vanish?'

I shake my head.

'Oh, Hephzi, if he did, I'd know God loved us after all.'

Poor Rebecca. I never look back as I climb down the tree and race down the drive to Craig. I know she's watching, and I don't want to know how lonely I make her.

Craig's eighteenth party on Bonfire Night is going to be even better than the one he had at his house in September. This time it's a proper do with a DJ and a buffet in the rugby club in the next village, there's going to be fireworks too. I've never seen a fireworks display, but I don't say that because that would be weird.

Pam is coming to the party, and her boyfriend, who

Craig hates, and his big brother Jamie. They treat me like I'm one of the family and we all pile into Pam's boyfriend's car and drive there together. I have to squeeze in the middle in the back and Craig keeps his arm tight round my waist. I haven't given him his present yet, I told him it's something special and he'll have to wait until later, so I think he's guessed already what it is.

I know what I'll have to do with Craig so he knows I really love him. When I was younger I found a book when I was nosing where I shouldn't and the photographs branded themselves indelibly on the back of my mind. Fingers of shame crept under my clothes, hot and sour as I flicked through the pages and even though I dared myself to look again I stayed away from my father's study after that. The thought of my parents doing those things made me sick, so I never told anyone, especially not Rebecca. I always wonder, though, how many more secrets the vicarage holds tight in its walls, whether it blushes or grins or hides its eyes in horror.

It seems like the whole sixth form is at Craig's birthday bash and I'm glad I look good. Girls I've never spoken to before say hi to me and admire my dress and my hair. Pam lent me her straighteners and Craig gave me the money for the dress and took me into town when I should have been in Chemistry to buy it. It's the nicest thing I've ever owned. Low cut, short and tight, I look like I could be in a magazine. I didn't dare show Rebecca though, she'd only have told me I looked like a slut. She has no idea what people wear, anyway, she's like an old sack of rags. Craig suggested I invite her along but I didn't tell her that in case she'd have said yes and, let's face it, that would have spoilt the whole thing. Craig and I dance, then I dance with Jamie, then with girls from college. People keep telling me what a great couple Craig and I are and I don't stop grinning.

Everyone goes outside for the fireworks and Craig holds me tight as they burst like hundreds of tiny bombs exploding in the sky. It's beautiful. When the others all go back in to carry on dancing, Craig and I hold hands and run further out into the night.

'I love you,' I tell him in the darkness and he kisses me dizzy in the field behind the club. The ground is a bit damp but we don't care and fall on to the grass.

That's when it happens. I'd thought it would hurt but it didn't. He was gentle, he knew I was a virgin. Ages ago I'd told him and asked if he was too, but he shook his head. 'But that was before I met you,' he'd said, 'if I'd known about you I'd have waited.' I didn't ask more but soaked my pillow with my tears that night.

Afterwards we go back inside and I wonder if anyone can tell. I hide in the loos for ages, resting my hot face against the cold wall of the cubicle. I tell myself not to be silly and put on more lip gloss, almost the last of it, and paint my smile back on, although it doesn't feel real any more. I don't know why.

When I come out I see Craig dancing with Daisy.

They're way too close, like they were that first night in the pub. I watch and they don't pull apart, she hooks her arms round his neck and leans forward to whisper something in his ear. I don't like the sad way he laughs and looks around, as if he's scared others are laughing at him too.

Once the party's over we go back to Craig's house. Pam invites me to stay but I shake my head and she kisses me on the cheek anyway and goes off to bed with her bloke. Craig and I sit in the lamplight of the living room. He stares at me for a long time then lights a cigarette and sits back on the sofa, taking his arm from round my shoulder.

'You're quiet. What's up?'

Things don't feel the same between us. He sounds cross with me.

'You don't regret it, do you?'

I shake my head, even though I feel a bit like crying. I'd thought I'd feel different, that I'd be grown up now. Instead I'm just even more scared. I chew my nail, wondering what I'm supposed to say.

'I didn't hurt you, did I?'

I shake my head again and he pulls me to him and kisses me as if that's the only thing that makes me happy. He smells of cigarettes and Daisy's perfume. I pull back.

'Will you take me home now?'

He sighs and gets up without waiting for me and goes and starts his bike. I sit on the back and have to hold tight. I hope the wind will whisk the tears from my eyes before he sees them. I get off in the dark corner round the back of the vicarage and wish I didn't have to scale the tree but know there's no choice. Tonight I wait until he's gone though, not wanting him to see me, suddenly realizing I must look like a fool. I wonder how long it will be before he tells me that we're over.

Rebecca

After

Stupid me.

It turned out that Hephzibah was right. I'd been getting cocky. Of course I'd be found out. Of course there would be retribution. How could I possibly think that I could go AWOL for a whole day and get away with it? Later that night, splenetic with drink, he took his revenge. The Father rang Mrs Sweet at the care home and told her that it was summer flu. I heard them hauling away the beds in our room, heard him laugh, sick with hate, before they threw me back in. But now there was nowhere left to hide, nowhere to play invisible. The room echoed and moaned and somewhere in the silent shadows I heard someone's baby start to cry.

'Shhh,' I pleaded, but the mewling wouldn't stop so I screwed my eyes tight against the straining wallpaper and blocked my heart to the noise.

The Mother gathered up my clothes, everything she could find, which wasn't much. I tried to hold on to the blue jumper but it ripped and tore as she wrestled it from my arms, the threads snapping and unravelling between us. They emptied the drawers in the chest of their paltry contents and scooped up the remains of Hephzi's contraband make-up, the bangles her friend Daisy had lent to her and that I'd never returned. They didn't find the silver chain and her perfume though, I'd put them under the loose boards in the corner under the window and so far they stayed safe. Then they left me in there, with barely enough food and water. There was no light and nowhere to go to the toilet. They left me for as long as they could, keeping me just almost alive. My hearing aids had broken entirely this time, he'd ground them under his shoe, and I lay there, in my pile of filthy blankets, scarred by my parents' hate, deaf to the possibility of hope. Hephzi was no comfort. Angry and afraid, she was hiding now and there was just that oozing stain on the wall for company.

The babies cried on and I thought I ought to sing to them. Searching for a tune, I found only despair.

One day he would go too far and I would die too. I could see it coming, a juggernaut rolling fast towards me and I knew I couldn't let that happen, not before I'd lived at least a fraction of my life. I crawled over to the window and pulled myself up to the sill to peer out. He hadn't thought to put on bars or even a lock – I could still open that window and leap out if I wanted to badly enough. Oh, I wanted to. But I was too weak and the fall would finish me off. I knew he wanted to break me so that I would stay here, a slave and a sycophant for the rest of my life.

I won't. I won't.

The week faded, grey and black and brown. The sky outside the window was concrete, as hard as heartbreak. I wondered where the summer had gone; perhaps the sun had died too. My room began to stink after only a couple of days. Headaches came and went and I drifted in and out of sleep. Sometimes it was light and sometimes it was night and the longer I went with such a small amount of food and water the more I knew I couldn't get out of the window. If only I could have heard something, listened out for noises downstairs and known that I hadn't been abandoned. I wondered where Mrs Sparks was, or the postman perhaps; there was a chance that he might miss me, wasn't there? I wondered if the whole village had perished and I was the only survivor of some terrible holocaust. Crawling to the door, I tried the handle. It was still locked. I could rot here, be gnawed to pieces by rats, and no one would ever come to find out what had happened to the girl with a face like fear.

Long ago in the past, far away from his madness, I'd understood for the first time what I really was. We'd been at our gran's and we'd helped her to make a cake and then played skipping outside, taking it in turns to turn the rope for one another. Hephzi had got it straight away, her plaits flying, her cheeks pink with air and fun. It had taken me longer and I stumbled over the rope, clumsy and stupid, but Granny had been patient and in the end I managed five skips in a row.

It was growing dusky and a little chilly so Granny took

us indoors and settled us on the sofa with hot chocolate and slices of the cake we'd helped to bake.

'I'll just be a minute, girls, doing the tea. You sit tight and do this little job for me.'

She handed us a huge book, heavy and thick, its pages crackled and rustled when we opened it. 'Here,' she said, 'find a fresh page and see if you can't stick these in for me, there's good girls.'

'What is it?' I asked Hephzi, who'd immediately snatched the bundle. She crowed with delight.

'Pictures! Pictures of us, look!' She thrust the first one under my nose. 'Look how pretty I am! And in this one!'

She scattered them everywhere, those pictures of us, photographs Granny must have taken on our trips out with her, some at the farm, some at the park. I smiled in all of them, big ugly grins, and I recognized at last what they all saw so clearly. My six-year-old self picked up those pictures and started to rip. I tore and I scrumpled, I scrunched and I threw. Hephzi started to shout and then to scream as I shredded the evidence of what I was.

'Granny! Granny! Come quick, Rebecca's tearing it all up. Granny!'

Granny came running and scooped me up like I weighed nothing at all and at once I stilled my flailing hands and let her hold me safe.

'Why did you do that, love?' she asked me later, quietly so that Hephzi wouldn't wake.

I couldn't answer her and shook my head.

'You mustn't destroy things, you know, those were my special photos of my special girls.'

'No,' I muttered.

'What?'

'No. You can see in the pictures, you shouldn't look at them. I'm a bad girl.'

'No, you're not. Now, don't be silly.'

I didn't answer and she understood.

'You're perfect, my love, different but perfect neverthe-less, you can't help how you look, it's not your fault. Do you understand me, Rebecca? Do you understand what I'm saying?'

She told me I had a syndrome. I asked if you could catch it, like a cold, and if it went away when you got bigger.

'No,' she said, sadly. 'No, I'm sorry, my love.' She said that it was called Treacher Collins. That the bones in my face hadn't formed properly when I was in my mother's womb and that's why I looked a little bit different.

'But Hephzi's my twin. She doesn't look like me. Why don't I look like Hephzi? We should be the same.'

I waited patiently on her knee for an explanation. She couldn't even begin to unravel the mystery for me; I was too little to follow what she said. All I knew was that I'd never change.

'But you're still perfect, you're still a wonderful little girl. Do you understand?'

Even if I did, it didn't matter. Even though she'd explained what was wrong with me and given it a name, even though she said I wasn't the only one, The Parents had decided who I was and I wore their loathing like a badge.

After that weekend, back when we'd been six and Granny had told me all about myself, I'd heard Granny try to threaten him. She said she'd call Social Services and have them take me away. She said she'd take me away herself. It was four years before they let us see her again.

Now, in my room, locked up and slowly dissolving, I traced my face with my fingers and felt it grow wet with my tears.

I woke another day to find sunlight flickering in at the window and I crawled over and peered out to see that the tree was still green after all, it was still growing. It reminded me of life and I wanted mine. I watched the drive, straining to see round the corner of the house and up the long gravelled path that led to the front door.

I knew that I was fading. I knew that I could not linger forever, waiting to be saved. But I did not want The Father to have his wish and I held fast to what was left. It was too soon to die. Another five days must have gone by, perhaps June was becoming July, before I spotted movement at last. A figure was coming up the drive. I couldn't see more than that but I knew it wasn't The Parents. The walk was different and I started to hope. My mouth formed the word *Danny* and maybe I breathed it into the silence as if it might grow and run out to meet him. I placed my palms on the glass and wondered.

After the figure retreated, a few minutes later, I realized what I should have done. I should have opened the window and called out, hollered for help. How stupid I was. I didn't need Hephzi to remind me.

I waited for Danny to return, watching at the window, determined not to miss my chance again. No one came. Then on Sunday they unlocked the door as if to let me out but pushed me into the bath and blasted the cold water from the shower on to my skin, which was to be disinfected and cleansed. The bottles stood ready. The Mother averted her eyes as she scrubbed and he looked on, intoning his sinful prayers. I screamed and she hesitated. He grabbed my head and plunged it under the water. Again and again and again.

Granny had told me never to hate. If you hate, you lose who you are. You mustn't hate the children who stare or the adults who point, the sneerers and sniggerers, the gawpers and grinners. *They're just ignorant, love, and not worth your tears.* I believed her then. Now I didn't know if I could help myself. I wanted to hate them so much it hurt more than anything else.

They gave me a pair of old pyjamas, too small for me and falling to pieces, second-hand cast-offs not even good enough for the charity bag. They'd taken everything else. My teeth clattered in my head and I wrapped my arms tight round myself as the sound of my own screams and the screams coming at me from the walls grew into a cacophony of fear. I backed away, into a corner and stared in horror at the bubbling and groaning paper behind where Hephzi's bed had stood, I saw it balloon and stretch and felt the end of something approach.

And then I saw Hephzi. She was there, suddenly, just for a moment, a dancing shadow at the window.

It's time, she says. *Run now. The door is open, run for your life, my sister. Run!*

Hephzi

Before

When you tell someone you love them, aren't they supposed to say it back? I guess not. In those books Rebecca reads I suppose it doesn't always happen like that, but I thought I'd be different, lucky. I thought Craig felt the same.

He doesn't show up at college until Thursday and the week is agony. I don't eat or sleep thinking about what I've done and wondering what he thinks of me now. Maybe he thinks I'm a slag, that's what everyone says about girls who sleep around, but I've only been with Craig. I pray he hasn't told anyone but I imagine people are looking at me and talking behind my back. Rebecca tells me not to be stupid when I ask her if people are whispering about me. Of course, I haven't told her what happened, although she'll have guessed. I know she's worked it out. The look on her face on Sunday morning said it all. I might as well have written it across my forehead.

When Craig finally slopes into the common room at break on Thursday I ignore him, even though my heart judders like it's about to break down. It's hard to look cool when you're sitting on your own so I pretend to be reading my Chemistry textbook and hold my breath waiting for him to come over and make it all better. But Daisy grabs him as he's walking by the lockers and I can see out of the corner of my eye that she's got her arm tucked in his and is tossing her hair and smiling with all her teeth. Stuffing my book into my bag I gather up my things and walk out. It's supposed to be a dignified exit but I don't reckon I've pulled it off, I'm sure I hear someone snigger as I leave.

Stupid me. I thought I could escape, I thought there was a chance for me and I'd make it out. I hide in the toilets for the afternoon, staring and staring at the wall until I think my eyeballs might explode.

Rebecca waits for me after college and we walk home. She sees my red eyes but says nothing the whole way, playing the sphinx.

Later that night, after we've gone through the charade of dinner with our parents and are supposedly studying in our room, I sit at the window wondering if I should sneak out and go and confront him. It's a cold and rainy November night and the wind's whipping up the tree, its branches are thrashing like it's in pain and the leaves are falling fast. I open the window and lean out to let the rain trickle on to my face. I lean so far that half my body's hanging over the sill. If I just let myself fall then all this would be over.

'What are you doing?'

I ignore my sister. I wish she'd disappear, she's constantly pushing at me, trying to get in my head, wanting to know.

'Shut the window. I'm freezing.'

'No.'

Rebecca comes over and tries to pull me in and we struggle for a bit before I give in. The window slams shut, only just missing my head, and I push Rebecca over and she looks at me like I'm nuts.

'What's the matter with you? Have you fallen out with that boy or something?'

She hates saying his name. She's such a cow.

'No. Why would I?'

'Well, why else are you so miserable?'

'I can be miserable if I like. Mind your own business.'

I sit on my bed and wish I had my own bedroom and my own space. I wish I were anywhere but here.

'You should get over it. Or make it up with him. I can't bear this.'

I think about what Rebecca says and wonder why we have fallen out. I haven't done anything, I've given him what I thought he wanted. The problem is mine, I realize. It's because he didn't say he loved me and that's what I thought the deal was. I thought if I had sex with him the result would be that he'd love me, but it didn't add up like that and I've been blaming him ever since. He doesn't realize how urgent it is that he loves me, how soon I need him to say it so we can move on and move in together. I get up and open the window again. If I don't go now I might lose him for good.

By the time I get to Craig's I'm like a drowned rat. Pam opens the door and stares at me as if I'm crazy before ushering me inside and grabbing towels and a dry jumper and jeans.

'Is Craig home?' I stutter through my chattering teeth.

'No, love, but I'll ring him on his mobile. See when he'll be back. Have you two had a falling out, then?'

I shake my head, then nod, not at all sure, before I start to blub like a baby. Pam hugs me like my mother never has and I wonder if I need Craig at all; Pam could just adopt me, that'd be enough. Craig would have all the time he needed to fall in love with me then.

I hear her whispering on the phone in the kitchen and hope she's not saying something bad. Maybe she's telling him I'm a loser and that he should dump me. I dunno.

She comes back into the living room with a cup of hot chocolate. I drink it fast, it is delicious, the nicest thing I've ever drunk. When every bit is gone and I've licked the mug clean I realize she's been staring at me, a bit bemused. I laugh and run my fingers through my straggly damp hair.

'Sorry, I was thirsty.' I don't tell her it's the first time since I was twelve that I've had hot chocolate and that it was always my favourite. Granny made it with marshmallows and whipped cream.

'D'you want some more?'

I nod. This time I sip more slowly, trying not to look like I've just landed from Mars.

'Craig's on his way back, love. He won't be long.'

'Where is he?'

She looks uncomfortable for a moment then turns on the telly. We sit watching *EastEnders* together, and I'm so engrossed I barely notice when Craig walks in.

'All right?'

He stands in the doorway looking at me. Straight away Pam jumps up and leaves us to it. I give him a smile, although it's a watery one, I can still taste rain and tears on my lips and Craig sort of smiles back.

'What's up?'

He's too nonchalant and still just standing there. This isn't how it used to be. Last week he would have hugged me and kissed me and told me I looked nice even if I were a mess. Taking a huge breath I speak.

'I thought I'd come over.' He cocks an eyebrow, waiting, so I try again. 'I missed you,' I say.

'Really? Seems to me that ever since the other night you've been avoiding me.'

'I haven't!' He frowns because he doesn't believe me. 'Why d'you think that? Please, Craig, I haven't been avoiding you. I swear.'

'All right. So you haven't been avoiding me. What else?'

'What d'you mean?'

'Well, what have you come here for? What else have you got to tell me?'

I have no idea what he wants me to say and sit staring at my hands. The *EastEnders* theme tune plays in the background. We're definitely finished. I don't know why he wants me to say it, why I have to be the one. Rebecca was right about him all along, he's a stupid pig. He got what he wanted and now he's acting like we've never met. Suddenly I'm more angry than sad and I stand up and look him in the eye; it's the look I give my mother when I want her to know how much I hate her.

'Screw you, Craig. Screw you.'

I push past him back into the rain. His mum's jeans bag around my waist and thighs and I clutch at myself as I start to run back the way I'd come only half an hour ago. I don't know if I'm crying or not, the rain streaks my face, lashes at my clothes, weighing me down, trying to pull me under. As I run I mutter and swear, naming all the things I'd do to Craig if I could, all the names I'd like to call him, all the ways I'd like to hurt him. Cars roar by as I run down the main road, sending up fountains of water. Then a bike screeches up beside me, the headlights blare into my face and I shield my eyes from the glare and stop, panting, still raging.

'What the hell's the matter with you?' he growls.

I don't see what right he's got to be angry with me.

'Leave me alone!'

I forge onwards, pushing past, but he's off the bike and grabbing me and holding me tight.

'What's going on, Hephz? What's your problem?'

'I haven't got a problem!' I scream into his face. 'You're

the bloody problem, you two-faced, evil, mean, pighead, shit . . .' Shuddering with sobs I can't finish my harangue and I collapse against him. All the misery of the past week comes pouring out and my tears are a torrent of sadness. He holds me for ages even though we're both getting drenched. The branches of the horse chestnut can't keep us dry and raindrops pool between us.

Still snivelling I pull away. 'Sorry.'

'No worries. Are you going to talk to me now or what?'

'I have to get home. They'll murder me if they know I've been out.'

Craig sighs and rubs the rain from his face. I run the short distance back home and slither my way up my tree and inside. Rebecca stares at me.

'What are you wearing? Where on earth have you been? You've been ages.'

'Did they notice?'

She shakes her head and I relax, pulling off the sopping clothes and draping them over the cold radiator in the hope that they might dry. Really they need wringing out in the sink but I daren't risk it.

'Did you find him?'

My nod isn't enough for her.

'What happened?'

'Nothing.'

'Oh, really? Then why've you been crying?'

'Get lost, Rebecca. Stop living your life through me, would you? If you want something interesting to think about then sodding well get your own boyfriend. And leave me alone.'

She shuts up. We go to sleep. I hope tomorrow is a better day.

When Craig and I should be at college the next day we drive to the coast instead. He picks me up as I'm walking to school and I leave Rebecca standing there like a lemon as we circle round and zoom out of the village. It's freezing and we huddle inside Craig's jacket under the pier. He tells me everything. It turns out that while they were dancing at his party Daisy had told Craig I'd been sleeping around. At first he hadn't believed her but she'd insisted and even found someone to back up her story. Samara. I knew I shouldn't have trusted her. If I hadn't gone round to Craig's last night and acted so crazy he'd still have believed her. As it was, he'd figured out that something didn't quite add up. Eventually.

So we're back together and Daisy is as sick as a pig. I'm never speaking to her again, I hate her. Craig agrees but he still hasn't said he loves me even though I've had sex with him again. Actually, I've done it quite a few more times. It's better than I thought it was going to be after the first time, when it was basically just uncomfortable, and we sneak off back to his house when we should be at college and spend the day in his bed. It's nice. He brings me cups of tea and we smoke cigarettes and he plays his guitar. He hasn't mentioned me moving in yet but I'm trying to be patient and playing it cool.

I can't believe I keep getting away with it. Each day when I wake up I wonder if today's the day I'll be found out. But then, because I'm so happy and so almost free, I forget to worry and just carry on being a normal girl, doing normal things and falling in love.

Rebecca

After

Almost blind with panic, I ran out of the vicarage. I hadn't known I could run like a cheetah, I hadn't known I was so quick. Out of the room I crept, and down the stairs, first one flight and then another, swift and light, invisible in the growing darkness.

Shadows flickered on the walls and the ceiling glinted with the last of the day's sun. I could just about see where I was going and fixed my eyes ahead, towards escape.

But I went too fast. In the hurry my feet tumbled over one another and I tripped down the last five stairs and on to the cold stone floor of the hall. *Get up, get up, come on*, I told myself and my legs lifted me again and I hurried to the heavy front door. It was hard to turn the key in the lock and I battled with the stiff, cold metal, trembling at the noise I imagined it made as it scraped a goodbye. Fumbling in my haste I was taking too long and I gathered all my strength to pull back the locks, wincing at the shunt and clunk of bolts drawn back and the moan of hinges as they cursed my departure. This house had been my prison for too long.

I threw back the door and shot out into the night. I hadn't believed it was really still summer outside and the warm evening air felt like a kiss. I launched myself on to the path which led away, through the trees and under the stars, into the world beyond.

The gravel hurt my bare feet but I moved faster for it as I fled down the path and ran like a shadow on fire towards the pavement, wild and free, but nearly so weak I could have lain down there and then and slept for as long as it took to be new. Then, at the gate, I stopped just for a moment and turned. The vicarage loomed massive behind me, its door still open, a gaping mouth that led to the very depths of my past and would swallow me whole given one last chance. Suddenly, more afraid than I could bear, my legs wobbled and I thought they might give. *But you're stronger than that!* I heard the wind whisper as a light flickered on and shadows moved at a window. They were coming. If they were to catch me! Adrenalin surged straight to my heart at the thought and I ran for the home next door, the only place I knew to go. It was dusk, the residents would be in bed and I prayed Danny would be there.

Suki opened the back door and I fell inside, unable to speak or breathe. Faces crowded me and I collapsed away from them into myself on to the floor. My legs had turned to water and I was a pool of fear. Someone gathered me up and lifted me to the day room, and I knew it was Danny by his strength. Around me and behind me the commotion buzzed and hummed. I was still unable to hear a thing but I felt the crowd gathering round me, questioning. Finding a last ounce of strength I looked up from Danny's arms and then I saw them. They had come for me. I caught a glimpse of their faces, puce with rage, yet still smiling through the blood. They stood there, talking at the door. They were pointing at me and talking so fast that I couldn't read what they said. Danny put me down and faced them, blocking their way through.

The room stilled. I peered through my fingers to try again to read The Father's lips.

'This is just dreadful. We do apologize,' The Father was saying. 'Rebecca's ill, delirious, we'll take her home and call the doctor.'

'She's a little terror, you know, our Rebecca,' The Mother added. 'You know how troublesome teenage girls can be!' I saw The Father shoot her a look, telling her to shut up and that he would handle this. She gaped her rictus grin.

Danny remained where he was, his back a barrier between them and me. I prayed he was strong enough to hold them off and that he understood that he was the only person standing between me and disaster. I'd seen The Father get his own way too many times to underestimate his power. He took a step forward, holding out his arms, and smiled, oh so sincere. I read my name on his lips again. He would fool Danny and take me back, say I was mad, tell any lie. I had to stop it. And now I knew I could.

When I spoke, Danny swung round.

'Don't let them take me. Please. Danny, don't let them.'

He nodded straight away. As they surged forward he put out his arms, stepping back to throw up a wall around me, a barricade of love as strong as steel. Here were the arms of the father I'd never known and I sheltered behind them as other hands, the hands of my friends, Suki and Michaela, and the boss, Mrs Sweet, held The Parents away. They must have realized that there were too many people for them to overcome and, as heads turned to hear sirens coming towards us, they melted into the walls, running from everything that they had done, the consequences they now had cause to fear. Some kind soul had called for an ambulance. I was lucky, this time it wouldn't be too late.

'Have they gone?' I whispered to Danny.

'Yes, yes, you're fine. They've gone. What happened?' His face was shocked.

'I don't know. Don't ask. Please?' I whispered through my dry, cracked lips. I coughed to clear my throat and let my head droop.

I wondered if I ever would tell.

Hephzi

Before

When we break up for the Christmas holidays I get sick. I wonder if I'm just homesick for Craig, but it's worse than that, it's horrible; I feel weak and dizzy all day long and the sight of the food Mother cooks sends me running for the bathroom every time. But I still have to work, helping with the chores, preparing the church for the Christmas events, posting newsletters, attending the meetings and Advent services, cleaning the vicarage. Father works us harder than he ever has before. It's like now we don't have the excuse of college, he's making up for every lost minute. Rebecca and I barely pause to breathe or eat, there's always something else that needs doing. She covers for me when I feel really bad and sometimes I get to sneak upstairs and have a nap. But by the evenings I usually start to feel better and when I hear Craig's bike out on the road I pull myself out of bed and edge my way down to him. For some reason he's fallen out with his mum and so we have to sit in pubs or at the bus stop. The sooner I move out the better. Maybe we could get our own place.

Craig asks me why I keep being sick. I explain that it's probably just a virus.

'You're on the pill, aren't you?' he says. I have no idea what that means and so I nod quickly. His face instantly brightens. 'Must be a bug then.' And I nod again.

Later I ask Rebecca what he meant. She shakes her head and looks more worried than ever.

I long for the Christmas holidays to be over. We get so busy attending services that I don't have the chance to sneak off and see Craig and I worry that he might come and knock on the door, like he's threatened to when I've said I can't see him. He's made up with his mum and she wants my parents to go over to hers for mulled wine and mince pies. I say no and Craig looks upset.

'How about you come over on Christmas Day, then?' he suggests. 'I haven't seen you properly for ages. I could ask Mum if you could stay the night, I reckon she'd be cool about it. What do you think?'

'No. I can't do that.' I'm nearly crying. I know that's stupid but everything makes me blub right now.

'All right. Whatever you say. Just don't cry though? OK?'

I snivel and smile though I want to have a mega bawl. If only I had the courage to tell him my idea about me moving out for good, but if he shot me down and told me no, then that'd be worse than anything.

He shows up one night, the day before Christmas Eve, and I hear his moped puttering on the corner and lean out of the window to shoo him away. It's way too dangerous, Saint Roderick and Mother Maria are downstairs with a whole load of their cronies, Mrs Sparks and the gang, and he's sober and alert, sipping tea and playing holy-holy. He's excited because he's almost important for once, and I'm supposed to be down there too, being Little Miss Perfect. He could be up any minute to drag me back to my duties. But Craig calls out that if I don't go down he'll come up, so I have to slither out of the window. I swear as I clamber hurriedly down the tree, snagging my clothes and tangling my hair.

'What is it?'

'Charming.' He grins at me, determined not to be offended. I let him have a kiss.

'Here.' He fumbles in his pocket and thrusts a little box at me, a flat square box and I grab it out of his hand.

'Shall I open it?'

'No. It's for Christmas Day. Since you won't come over I thought I'd better do a special delivery.'

'Thanks,' I whisper, holding the package like someone might be about to snatch it from me.

'You're welcome. See you, then.'

I watch him go, sorry I have no present of my own, determined to open the box as soon as I can.

The silver chain with my initial hanging from it flows like magic in my hands. I swear I'll never take it off and fasten it round my neck, sure it has special powers, sure that it's a sign.

But the next day is Christmas Eve. And, despite all my protests, Craig shows up for the midnight mass with Pam. I can't believe he's done this. I've told him time and again not to come near the vicarage or the church, and here he is, slouching in and smiling at me. He's wearing a smart over-coat I've never seen before and he looks handsome and older. I feel my heart beating in my ears and the pew begins to tilt beneath me, as if the world is spinning out of con-trol, no longer suspended perfectly in the universe but falling fast towards the sun. Rebecca has seen them too and our eyes lock. We both understand that we are caught in the grip of something awful and that the catastrophe has come. Then Mother prods me upright with her sharp elbow and swings her head round, sensing and smelling my anxiety, and I know she knows. Her eyes settle on Pam and Craig sitting a few rows behind us and when Pam smiles at her she snaps her head forward again, her eyes wide and staring at my father. There's going to be trouble later.

Father starts the service. He intones the prayers in his usual Christmas Eve-y way; he loves this service because so many people actually come, even if some of them are tipsy from the pub, and he makes his sermon extra long, probably to punish them for not showing up from one year to the next.

'The birth of the Christ child is a moment of joy to be shared. We welcome you here to this service, to share in that joy. In all our lives the arrival of a child is a blessing of such magnitude that it can barely be expressed. But the birth of the baby Jesus, come to redeem sinners, to pay for the heavy burden of humanity, is a gift beyond man's understanding. To make the sacrifice of oneself, to be last, not first. That is what Jesus Christ the simple, humble baby taught and it is a lesson we all must learn.'

So he goes on, reaching forward to the congregation with his arms aloft. He usually manages to keep the devil out of it at Christmas, but this year he can't resist. I think it's especially for me because he fixes me with his stare as he licks his lips and continues.

'So praise be to God for sending His child to save us from the devil within. Praise be that He came to save us from the allure of lust, from the glitter of greed and the sleep of sloth. Let us confess our sins as one here tonight and leave this church renewed in our faith, more determined to banish the devil and his desires from our hearts. Let us go forth and celebrate Christmas, deaf to the beat of the devil's drum.'

He's on a roll tonight. I think I'm going to be sick.

A few Amens are muttered and the choir launches into a hymn. My favourite's always been 'Away in a Manger', I sang it once, a solo, but they're not singing that tonight and I can't join in. My lips barely move and nor do Rebecca's. She grips my fingers tight in hers, as if there's no point caring any more if he sees or not.

I don't dare look round again.

When the choir eventually finishes the final hymn, I grab Mother's hand and scurry out of the church before Pam has a chance to descend on us. I can see that she's clutching something bottle-shaped and guess that she's brought it as a Christmas gift for my parents. Oh God. If she speaks to them then that's it, our secret's out and everything's over. It's too soon, I'm not ready. I haven't packed or decided how to leave. And Rebecca, what will she do if I run away? I drag Mother with me, back to the vicarage, and Rebecca hurries along still holding my hand. But this is not right, this is not allowed, we ought to be outside the church bidding the congregation farewell and a Merry Christmas too, playing our assigned parts. Instead we cower behind the front door of the vicarage. Mother stares at me.

'What's going on?'

'Nothing.'

'Then what do you think you're playing at?' She pushes at me, trying to get past, but I stand firm.

'Nothing.'

She turns to Rebecca. 'What's going on here?'

Reb stays silent and earns a sharp slap to the cheek. Then the front door heaves and I tumble to one side. He walks in. I can't believe it, he's smiling and my own mouth lifts for a second in relief. Then I realize what it really means and I shrink behind my sister, whose fragile body is braced like a shield. Behind him come Pam and Craig. We all stand together in the hall.

'Maria, this is Hephzibah's boyfriend, Craig, and his mother, Pam.' Mother steps forward and takes her hand and smiles like a normal human being. I know he's invited them back just to make me shake a bit longer and I can't bear it. I want them to go right this minute. I want to get my things and go with them. Rebecca can come too.

Pam is smiling at me, really pleased. She's been desperate to meet them. Why wouldn't they stay away, like I told them to?

'Craig and Hephzibah have been seeing each other for quite some time, Maria, or so Pam tells me.' I don't dare look at my father. 'You know, I thought something was going on – isn't it funny, Pam! One's children can be so secretive, but we parents understand them only too well.'

'Oh, yes, Craig's always been a bit like that too. But we love having Hephzi round, she's a lovely girl. You must be very proud of her.'

'Oh, indeed. Of course.' Father smiles and looks at me. So does Craig. I think he wants me to say something and I wonder what it should be. Should I offer to go and put the kettle on? Get out a Christmas cake my mother has lovingly baked, just for an occasion like this? Not likely. Instead I try to smile back at everyone but it wavers into a grimace on my lips. Rebecca grips my hand even tighter. She'd said this would happen but I thought I could make my plan work.

'It's been delightful to meet you, Pam. We'll see you again, I'm sure,' Father says. They don't hear the chill in his dismissal because they're off down the path, calling Merry Christmas, waving goodbye. *Goodbye, Craig*, I think. *Goodbye.*

The door shuts ever so quietly behind them. Father turns round. He takes us in, standing there in a row before him. There is a silence that is stiller and blacker than night and we wait for the bomb to explode. I am ready to run. The bottle Pam gave him hits the wall behind us and shatters; wine drips and runs like blood and all is noise at last. He doesn't pause to ask questions. Nothing could ever justify the infringement of his rules and he's not interested in hearing my excuses. No. He'll cut straight to the punishment. Christmas is come at last.

In the night I wake, it's too soon to be morning and for a moment I wonder what's wrong with me. Then I remember the beating and feel my swollen cheek, rotate my wrenched shoulder. Those pains are familiar; it's not that which has woken me. Then I feel the hot wetness between my legs. My period, finally, I think, and try to roll out of bed to clean myself up before the mess gets any worse. But then there's suddenly another great gush of it all down my legs and I hold myself right where he kicked me in the stomach as I double over in pain. Immediately Rebecca is beside me.

'Hephzi? Are you all right?'

'No.' I can hardly speak or breathe and I crumble on to the floor. I hear her gasp as she switches on the lamp and sees the blood. I hear her demand I tell her what she should do, but all I know is the pain. I wonder as I lie there why she doesn't go for some help, I'm sure she should, but I know she's afraid and as I bleed I wonder what is happening to me and what he has done.

'It's all right,' she says. 'It'll be over soon.' I don't know how she can know that when I don't understand what's wrong with me. I think I ask her, but she just tells me to shush, I think I hear her say that it's only a baby and that I'm not to worry, but I'm not sure how that could be true. She fetches a cold cloth to hold on my face and I wait to feel better.

But the pain gets worse and the dark night only grows longer as cramps creep down my legs. My bed is covered in towels and I lie there, beached and bleeding. I must be dying. No one ever said that this is how you die. I start to shiver and beg Rebecca for more blankets. She hovers over me, her face a tiny star somewhere near heaven.

I dream a bit of driving too fast with Craig and screaming as his bike tips and we topple towards a great black abyss. The dream jolts me awake again and I'm sweating and hot now and throw off the covers. When I vomit Rebecca is there holding me, telling me I'm OK. I know I'm not. She brings me water but I vomit again.

The night is so long.

'Reb, please, help me,' I say.

'What shall I do?' she asks again, but I need her to take charge. She's always protected me before. Why not now?

'Shall I call them?' she asks me and I nod. She disappears and then returns again but still alone. I cry because of the pain and because of everything else and then I forget who I am and where I'm going. Once I think I hear Craig's voice outside, shouting for me, and I sit up, startled, but it's only Rebecca holding water to my lips, begging me to drink as she mops the sweat from my face.

Daylight comes, grey and dull. We never did open a stocking, I think suddenly, not once. I hear them hollering for us to come, to get downstairs and go to church and Rebecca throws on her clothes, kisses me quickly and leaves. The bells are ringing, oh come all ye faithful, and I hear them leave without me. When the door slams and the house is empty I cry and wonder if I'll see her again.

It drags on. The blood keeps coming. I feel tired and weak and can't speak any more. I try to find a cold patch on my mattress, I need to rest, I need peace. Rebecca is back; she tends me. When night falls again a shadow drops over my bed. My father. I reach out my hand to him, look up into his face and whisper for help. He turns on his heel and leaves me there.

Someone calls an ambulance, I hear it wailing from far away.

PART TWO
Rebecca

She died of an infection. That's what they said. The blood she'd lost, the baby she'd left on our bedroom floor, that hadn't been what killed her. It had been the poison that had taken root inside and attacked her until she couldn't fight on. No one blamed The Father. No one interrogated The Mother. No one asked why they hadn't brought her sooner. If I hadn't called the ambulance she never would have made it to the hospital at all. I think she was already dead by the time it arrived.

Of course they blamed me. They told everyone I'd kept it a secret, kept her locked up there and pretended she had a touch of the flu to protect her because there'd been a row. Just a normal family spat, you know the sort. Of course they'd nipped in to check on her and she'd seemed all right and then, once they'd realized the situation, well, after that it had all been too fast, everything they'd done to try to help had been a moment too late. I watched The Mother shed her crocodile tears as she pointed the finger my way and the doctor shook his head and placed his hand on her shoulder in comfort. It was a tragedy, no one could have predicted how soon she would go, she really mustn't blame herself.

The morning after she died we went back to the vicarage and I cleared up the mess. The towels soaked in the bath, turning its grimy white porcelain red, flower after flower of crimson stained the floor and my hands as I dragged the sheets and the bedding across the hall and into the bathroom. He drank downstairs as I scrubbed. She sat in the kitchen worrying her prayers. We left Hephzi there in the morgue, cold and lonely, without even her baby for company. I wanted to creep back and stay with her, to hold her hand and tell her a story, but I didn't dare. Instead I waited out the hours in our room, my room, wondering if it had been a dream. A week after she died they held her funeral. They made me wear her dress and they cried sham tears. Everyone knew I was the one to blame.

No one ever told me and Hephzi about babies. We both found out the hard way.

I should have guessed she was pregnant when she was sick all the time and didn't get her period. Perhaps I did, but I was hiding it from us both. The funny thing is Hephzi liked little kids. I always thought they were annoying. When we'd been younger one of our tasks had been to mind the little ones while their parents were at one of The Father's prayer meetings or services. One of the mums usually hung around to keep an eye on us, it made them uneasy to see me touching their children, although they always talked to Hephz.

'You're good with babies. How about babysitting one

night for us?' one lady said. She was fairly new to the village and didn't know how things worked.

'Oh, thanks, that'd be great.' Hephzi was daft enough to think it was actually a possibility. My sister could hope for England.

'D'you want little ones, when you're older, you know, when you're married?' the woman continued. I tried not to roll my eyes.

'Maybe.' Hephzi paused. 'I don't know though. How'd you get a baby?'

The woman smiled a funny little smile. 'Oh, you should ask your mum, she'll tell you all about it.'

I guess she thought eleven-year-olds ought to have known the facts of life. But she must have told The Mother about their chat because later she scrubbed our mouths out with soap, making us gag and retch, as he looked on, and told us never to speak about that filthy business again. Hephzi hadn't been satisfied with that and she'd wondered and wondered. Maybe Granny would have told us if she'd had the chance. By the time we went to college everyone knew everything there was to know and no one thought to share the nitty-gritty. That was old news. Not to Hephzi though; we'd never studied Biology, never practised putting a condom on a banana. My mouth had dropped open when Archie told me about how they'd done that in Year Nine and how he'd even laughed about it later with his mum and dad.

All Hephzi knew about was the dirty thing, the thing

the Mother said we mustn't do because if we did we'd go to hell. The same with our periods. It was the devil in us that made us bleed every month. The blood was there, the devil's sign, to remind us, like my face, that we were rotten. I'd believed her for a while until Hephzi found out from a girl at a church group that it was all normal and just part of growing up. They'd whispered about it in the toilets during a meeting. Hephzi might have known she was going to hell for doing what she did with Craig but she didn't know she would have a baby. Poor little thing. Craig still has no idea and I'm never going to tell him.

After I escaped from the vicarage and made my mad dash to the care home, an ambulance came and took me to the hospital. Perhaps it was the same one that had taken my dying sister, six months before. Danny came with me. I clung on to his hand but he prised my fingers away and placed me on crisp, white sheets and let them give me medicine, bandage my body and put in a drip. They would keep me alive and I would survive. Hephzi should have made it here. She would have too, if only I'd called for help just a little sooner.

The nurses asked me questions but I kept quiet; there was no need to tell them, they wouldn't believe me, why should they? I'd seen it all before. Danny came back and I asked him not to leave me alone again and he nodded. Unless Danny was there The Father would turn up, he'd take me back to the vicarage and I'd never escape again. I think he understood that this was my only chance.

Danny said he was going to call the police but I shook my head so hard and told him I'd kill myself if he did, so he subsided into his chair like a great bear retreating back into its cave. He said he supposed it could wait, just until I felt better.

Someone else called them though. A policewoman showed up the next day with her notebook and questions. I pretended to be asleep. She didn't give up though, she came back every day until in the end I had to sit up and speak, just in the hope of getting rid of her.

'Rebecca, how are you?'

'OK.' I eyed her carefully. I didn't like the way she stared at me, I think she thought I was a nuisance.

'So, can you explain to me how you ended up here?'

'No.'

'Think back, the night you were hurt, what happened?'

This was ridiculous. The night I was hurt? To which night did she refer? I would never tell her. And her voice sounded cross already, I didn't want to make her any more angry with me and that was precisely what would happen if she thought I was telling lies. I simply shook my head.

'You don't need to be frightened, Rebecca, no one can hurt you now, you know.'

That's what she thought. She didn't know The Father. He'd killed Granny. He'd killed Hephzi. I was next on his list.

'You know the doctors showed me your X-rays. I've seen all the evidence. All I need is your word.'

I shrugged and she sighed and stood up to leave, turned and walked to the door, and then stopped.

'If anyone did to my kids what someone's done to you, well, I wouldn't be responsible for my actions, love. I've seen every scar, counted every fracture on your x-rays, old ones and new ones, I've heard about your bruises and how you scream when you sleep. I know you're scared, Rebecca, but you have to stop this. You have to be brave. I'll be ready when you are.'

For a moment she almost had me. I saw her with her kids, reading them bedtime stories, playing snakes and ladders on a rainy day, baking their birthday cakes. For a moment I was nearly convinced. But then I remembered how powerful he was. He'd get away with it, he'd lie his way out of my story and make them think I was mad. He would hand them the chains with which to bolt me down, just when I was about to be free. After all, a man of the cloth was more sacred than the law. His word was divine. Danny came again and again and tried to persuade me to speak but I wouldn't listen. For once I was going to do things my own way.

But then came the psychiatrist. And the social worker, then the students and the therapists, then the police-woman again.

She looked at me sadly. 'You're not still being silly, are you, Rebecca?'

I turned over to face the wall. It was cold and blank, it didn't bubble with secrets.

'If you tell me what happened then I'll make sure that whoever did this to you is punished. I'll make it so they can never hurt anyone again.'

She walked round the side of the bed, found my hand clenched round a ball of white hospital sheet and held it.

'Please, let me help you.' She disappeared in a blur of my tears, although I felt the pressure on my fingers as she squeezed cold comfort and spoke empty words.

I couldn't speak to these strangers and when the doctors prodded and poked, when they fitted me with new hearing aids and suggested surgery on my jaw and discussed me like I was no more than an unusual and rather fascinating problem, I pretended I was with Hephzi; me, Hephzi and Granny on the swings in the park with the pond, racing each other higher and higher, singing and laughing, out in the blue.

It was the day that Danny took me back to his house that the story finally came out. It was as if it had been waiting for its chance, waiting for a safe place to sneak out of hiding. I opened my mouth and the words spilled out like rats following the Pied Piper. Soon the room was swarming with the sounds of the plague I'd released. At the worst bits Danny slammed out of the room and I heard him smashing things in the kitchen but it didn't worry me. I knew he wasn't angry with us.

I didn't tell him about my baby though. Remember the deepest scars, the stories that I hide, the ones I can't explain? Some things are too shameful to show even to your friends. My baby had to stay back there, in our room, behind the paper. I wondered if Hephzi was looking after them and the fright hit me again, a shock like a sting to the heart. I hoped she was safe.

I'd known the second I saw Hephzi's face the day after Craig's birthday party. It was written all over her like a welt from a strap. She'd let him do it to her. *It*. The filthy thing.

'Don't look at me like that,' she'd said. 'Stop it, Rebecca!'

I said nothing, got up, made my bed and went down to start the chores. For me it was a day like any other; for her, well, it was different. She never told me how, she wanted to keep her secret.

Hephzi thought I knew nothing. She thought I was a blessed innocent. But I think for a long time I probably knew more than she did. As her body grew, I kept myself bony and childlike, wondering how long it would be before I could make myself disappear.

The Father didn't want me, he wanted Hephzi. It was obvious. I watched his eyes following her around rooms and saw how he sought out her curved, vital perfection. Though he slapped and snapped at her it never went too far; her nose remained unbroken, her ribs held her strong and straight, even her fingers still flexed, graceful and pretty. But when he stared at the line of her back and her beautiful white shoulders, her mouth and her chest, I'd distract him by doing something stupid so he'd remember to hate me instead of to hurt her.

One time it got too much. I told no one how it went that Sunday night when he was so drunk that a new rage erupted. I was only thirteen, still so scared of him, my heart bruised black and blue.

He'd made Hephzi sit on his knee and read to him. She was too big and her legs dangled over his, touching the floor. He liked the Old Testament best but Hephzi wasn't good at reading aloud, and the long words and ancient sounds made her stutter and stumble.

'Lam . . . lament . . . sorry, Daddy!' She found a smile and tried his face for forgiveness before she attempted it again, 'Lamentata ... lamenta ...' She coughed and looked over to me. I mouthed the word slowly to her, *Lam-en-ta-tions*, and she nodded, and got it right at last.

I watched his hand clench and flex and saw his finger stab again and again at the page as she kept getting words wrong. It was exhausting to strain against the tension, waiting for the strike. My body begged to collapse back against the chair, to deflate and shrivel, but my vigilance was all that would keep my sister safe. He drained his glass and then sent her for more and as she passed me my eyes told her not to return. Hephzi nodded and I waited to feel the creep of her feet on the stairs.

For a moment, after she left the room, The Father slumped and suddenly slept and I thought I could be free too, scuttle off and leave him to his stupor. But I must have been clumsy or made a noise because he jolted awake as the door betrayed my intentions with a Judas groan.

'Where is she?' he demanded, his voice thick, his eyes blinking rapidly.

'She went to bed. You fell asleep. Shall I read now?'

He shook his head wildly as if he were trying to escape a wasp buzzing in his ears and then lurched to his feet and advanced.

I should have run, but where to? I couldn't lead him upstairs, not to our room, not to where Hephzi was safe. Maybe I could have screamed but I knew no one was listening. The walls were thick and heavy and dumb.

He may have been drunk but still he was strong.

Ox-heavy, he handled me like I was meat. The door was shut fast again, it slammed finally as he lurched against it and grabbed my neck. The Mother had disappeared hours since and Hephzi slept just above our heads, oblivious.

I closed my eyes and felt the tearing, felt his thick weight on my back, the flesh of his hand shoved in my mouth so I couldn't cry or speak or shout. I never would have anyhow, I wouldn't have let him know the pain that spliced me in two and made my head spin in fainting arcs. The bruises on my thighs lasted weeks and it hurt me to walk but I kept the ugly secret hidden somewhere behind the wall.

When Hephzi's baby cried there, mine did too.

After that I felt old. Old and cold and stolen. I had no one to tell and no words to tell with. Hephzi wouldn't unearth what I'd buried; she hid from horror until it hunted her down.

But now he will never hurt me again.

Slowly I recovered. Archie slept downstairs on the sofa so that I could have his bedroom. I didn't feel enough to feel guilty, sensation had drained out of me when I'd told my story to Danny; he had taken it all on his shoulders and now when I saw him he looked dark and grim. I'd begged him not to tell, not to breathe a word to the police or a friend or anyone at all and he couldn't break my trust. Cheryl tried to convince me too but I begged them for time and reluctantly they agreed. Danny brought me books, piles of them, and left them by my bed, waiting for

me to read. I didn't have the will. After all that time yearn-
ing for stories I couldn't start a single line; the sight of the
pile depressed me and I turned again to face the wall,
evading the future.

What I did do though was sit with Archie's computer.
All night I tapped and tapped on the keyboard. I found
out everything they'd never told us. By the morning my
eyes would ache and Cheryl would shake her head as she
brought me my breakfast.

'What've you been up to, love? You look knackered.'

'Nothing. I didn't sleep well, that's all.'

'You get some kip now, then, sweetheart, you need your
sleep to mend.' She'd drop a kiss on my head and leave me
to it, hurrying off to work. Then I'd put the tray on the
floor and gorge myself on message boards, websites,
forums, places where I could ask all the questions for
which I'd never had answers. I found out everything I'd
never known about myself. Granny had tried to explain
but I'd never really understood. There were people like
me all over the world. Their lives had not been blighted;
they had homes and families and degrees and jobs. Yes,
people had laughed at them or called them names, but
they were survivors. I cried with relief.

I found out why I got a baby and why Hephzi did too.
Of course I knew it was the dirty thing that did it, but I
hadn't known about the egg and the sperm, that it was
simple biology, neither God nor the devil were crouching
inside, waiting to emerge. In fact it was all normal really,

normal and natural and not some sick secret. I groaned for Hephzi and what she'd lost. But when she'd been with Craig I thought it must have been different for her, that's what it seemed like anyway. I hoped it had been better. I listened for her to tell me but she said nothing.

'Hephzi? Are you here?'

She didn't answer and I swung my head around, searching the room, hoping she might be hiding somewhere after all. I wanted to talk.

'Please, Hephz, I need you. Please come out.'

Once upon a time she would have come when I'd called. But now. Nothing.

If she wasn't here, then where was she?

Once the bruises had faded, Archie came in every day to sit on the end of the bed and talk.

'All right?' he said, looking at me hopefully, even more freckly than I'd remembered. Even that didn't make me smile. I averted my eyes and scrunched under the covers but still he kept coming. I guessed Danny made him stick at it, kind of community service, or maybe he thought we could have some little pity party together. I told myself not to be bitter.

After a week of silence Archie grabbed one of the books, the one on the top of the pile, and started to read. Hearing him stutter and stumble over the words was too painful and I sat up, despite myself, and grabbed the book out of his hands.

'Here, I'll do it.' Ignoring his flushed face, I read until

my mouth was dry and my cheeks ached, and he sat and listened with his head resting on his fists, laughing or grimacing and totally held by the story. It was a good one, *Frankenstein*; I'd not read it before, I'd got nowhere near S for Shelley, and as I read I wondered if Archie saw the irony.

'What d'you mean?'

'Oh, nothing. Forget it.' But I was sorry for the Creature. They'd called him devil too. Archie agreed that it was sad he'd never found anyone to love him and then I pretended to be tired.

One day Archie told me it was now August outside. He pulled the curtains open and flung open the window. Cheryl did that every morning, although the minute she left the room I pulled them back tight against the light, but I let Archie have his own way. For a moment the sun felt good.

'You could come down. Dad's doing a barbie. Go on.'

His eyes looked so bright with hope, hope for me and hope that he would be the one to lure me out of the dark room and down into the sunny day, that I couldn't refuse.

'Give me a minute, would you?'

Cheryl had bought me clothes and left them in bags on the floor. Ungratefully I had never emptied those bags. Now I put my hand inside and pulled out the clothes. Brand-new clothes. Something I hadn't seen for over five years, since our twelfth birthday and Granny's treat, our special shopping expedition. There was a dress made of crinkly material and patterned with little flowers. It had thin straps and fell in soft folds to just above my knees. I held it against the pyjamas I'd been wearing for weeks. Unsure if I ought to, I yanked off the tags and pulled on new underwear and then the dress. My arms were bare, my legs too. That would never have been permitted and I felt half naked. Searching through the bags I found a little cardigan, it was pink with short sleeves. The mirror was in the hall. I would have to step out to see. If Hephzi were here she'd tell me how I looked, she'd be honest. I still needed her but she wouldn't come now. She'd been gone ever since I escaped and no matter how hard I tried to call her back there was never an answer.

Archie banged on the door, making me jump.

'You ready?'

'Yes, OK. I'm coming.'

He escorted me downstairs, holding my arm like I was some kind of invalid, I realized that must be how he saw me, and then presented me proudly to the rest of the family as if he'd just made a joyful discovery. I wished it was that easy, that an angel had rolled away the stone and I had been in fact reborn and remade. I wanted to be a better version of me, one with all wounds healed. But that doesn't happen in real life. In real life there's no resurrection, even if you wish for it every night.

I watched as they all bit back exclamations, all except Ben, who jumped up and covered me with a huge hug.

'I'm glad you isn't deaded now,' he said, and I realized I

was too. For a moment no one laughed and then I heard myself giggle.

'Me too, Ben. Thanks.' The ice was broken and Danny handed me a hot dog and Cheryl poured me a glass of Coke; the ice clinked as I raised my glass and said cheers with Ben over and over again until Cheryl told him to stop. I perched on a chair and listened to the family around me, everyone glowing in the sun.

I lasted half an hour that day and that was enough. Over the next few days and then weeks the time I spent out of my room gradually increased and we became used to each other. They never made me feel like a nuisance and I helped Cheryl with the cooking and cleaning when she'd let me.

One afternoon Cheryl took me with her to the supermarket to do the big shop.

'You help me choose, love,' she said. 'Get all your favourites.'

I didn't have favourites, I liked whatever she made and I told her so. But still she encouraged me to pick what I wanted and tried to chat and gossip as we went round the aisles. She thought if she kept me busy I wouldn't notice people staring. The shop was huge, like the belly of a great whale, and I was sure we'd never find our way out again. The rows and rows of food and clothes and shampoo and tellies and toasters and drink made me dizzy. We'd only ever used the local shop; this was the first time I'd driven to a store since our twelfth birthday.

Finally, able to think of something to ask for, I told Cheryl I'd like ice cream for dessert and she pelted off to find some. I lagged behind, gazing around me. A voice broke through my reverie.

'Rebecca?'

I recognized that voice immediately. I didn't want her to stop and talk to me.

'Rebecca, dear?' She put her hand on my arm and I paused and waited.

'How are you? Your parents told me you'd moved out. Where are you living now, then?' Her voice was heavy with concern, almost hushed with worry.

'I'm fine, Mrs Sparks, thanks. How are you?'

'I'm well, of course. Thank you for asking.'

'Well, I'd best go now.'

'Oh, of course, dear, but you know, you really ought to go and make things up with your parents – I hope you don't mind me saying, but they're devastated, you know. We're all praying for you.'

I nearly screamed then but remembered where I was just in time. *Have you heard this, Hephzi?* I called, but she gave no reply. Then Cheryl whizzed up, waving her list at me, calling that we ought to hurry. Mrs Sparks eyed her suspiciously.

The women waited to be introduced.

'Cheryl, this is Mrs Sparks. She lives in my village. She's a helper at the church.'

'Churchwarden, actually. I've known the girls, I mean Rebecca, all her life.'

'Oh, have you?' Cheryl's voice had taken on an edge. I grabbed the handle of the trolley and started to drag her off in the direction of the tills.

'I recognize you, I'm sure,' Mrs Sparks called after us. 'Aren't you the wife of the chap who works in the care home?'

'Don't answer her, Cheryl, she's a busybody, she'll tell them.'

'I want to give her a bloody piece of my mind,' muttered Cheryl. She stuffed the food into the thin plastic bags, hurriedly punched numbers into the machine, and I scurried after her as she marched back to the car. On the way home she broke the silence.

'What I don't understand is how all these people have just stood back all this time and watched you being treated so bad? I can't understand it. I can't.'

She wanted me to explain. I fiddled with my seat belt.

'I mean, it's not right, you can't let that kind of thing go on under your nose and do nothing about it. It's a bloody disgrace, is what it is.'

I thought about what she was saying.

'Mrs Sparks did help us, sort of. She gave us things, food, clothes. She tried to help.'

'Not bloody hard enough, Rebecca. You deserved better.'

Cheryl still didn't understand how clever The Father was, how good he was at putting on his mask, how well he kept Mrs Sparks in flattery and falsehoods.

'And as for your aunt and uncle, well, they're even worse. Your own flesh and blood, just leaving you like that with people I wouldn't let mind my cat, let alone two defenceless kids!'

Cheryl had been waiting a long time to get this off her chest. I let her talk on as we drove home. Nothing she said was a surprise to me, I'd had years and years to think the same thoughts.

'Auntie Melissa moved to Scotland. She couldn't really visit.'

'Not good enough, I'm afraid.'

'People don't bother, they want an easy life.'

'Well, they should be ashamed of themselves.'

Maybe so. It took too much energy to be angry though, I needed all my strength just to face the rest of my life.

I was almost as happy as I'd ever been living with Danny and his family. But I knew I couldn't sleep in Archie's room forever, it wasn't fair. I sat on the bed and tried to think of an alternative to the situation, but I had no bright ideas. I could really have done with my sister's input, she knew more about being normal than I did. Her answer had been to get a boyfriend, but that wasn't an option for me. I'd found a family, but they weren't really mine and there wasn't enough room. Even though I did the hoovering and helped make the dinner, I knew it wasn't much of a contribution and that I shouldn't outstay my welcome. It was time to go, again.

Then, at the end of the month, the phone went. I was

playing with Ben and thought nothing of it until Cheryl called that it was for me. I didn't like the look on her face when I took the receiver from her hand and she marched off into the kitchen, muttering under her breath. Holding the phone like I was handling a gun I whispered hello. At first I didn't recognize the voice on the other end of the line.

'Hello?' I managed again.

'Rebecca. It's your Aunt Melissa.'

There was a long pause while I processed the information. I could hear her breathing, too fast.

'Are you still there?'

I nodded but of course she couldn't hear that. My mouth was far too dry to speak.

'Well, Rebecca, if you're listening, I want you to know, I heard what happened, that you've left home, and, if you like, well, you're welcome with us any time.'

She waited for me to respond. Part of me wanted to tell her that she was too late, Hephzi was already dead and I'd managed to get out without anyone else's help.

'I'm sorry about it all. I should have done something sooner.' Her voice became agitated. 'She never should have married him, we told her at the time, but she was desperate, you know.'

'What do you mean?' I interrupted.

'Your mother. Oh, it's water under the bridge, but I'm sure it's all his fault, Roderick's.'

'No. Not all.'

'Yes, well, if you let me know, I'll be there whenever. Just give us a bit of warning. It's a bit of a drive.' She laughed nervously.

'How did you get this number?'

'Mrs Sparks, you know the church woman? She called me and let me know what had happened and where you were. I left my number when we were down for, you know, your sister's funeral.'

I thought about that and wondered what had been said. If Mrs Sparks had worked out where I was then maybe The Parents had too, maybe they'd be coming for me, quiet in the night, to stuff me in a sack and carry me off.

'I don't want to see you.'

'All right, that's fair enough. But I'd like a chance to talk to you, to explain a few things.'

'OK,' I whispered in the end. 'I'll let you know.' She reeled off her number and I scribbled it down and stuffed the paper into my pocket. I dwelt on the call all day and what she'd said about The Parents, deciphering her cryptic clues, filling in the words, completing the puzzle. But I couldn't get there on my own, there were still too many blanks.

I knew I had to leave Danny and Cheryl's, I wasn't their responsibility and their house wasn't made for so many people – it was starting to split at the seams and though Danny didn't seem to notice Cheryl looked harassed. But I didn't know how to leave or where to go next. Living with Auntie Melissa was out of the question. She'd left us to rot and what if The Parents showed up? I couldn't rely on Melissa and Simon to back me up and keep me safe. I retreated to Archie's room and stayed there all day. In the middle of the night I packed my things. Only after that did I fall asleep.

In the morning when the family came down for breakfast I was already ready to go, even though I still had no idea where. Cheryl stared at me as she stood halfway down the stairs, still bleary eyed and in her dressing-gown.

'What's up, love? What are you doing up and dressed at this time in the morning?'

I felt horrible making my announcement. 'I'm leaving today, Cheryl. I just waited, I mean, I wanted to say good-bye and thank you.'

'You what? You can't just up and off like that. Don't be so daft, come and get your breakfast.'

'No, really, it's time I went. You've been so kind.' Every word hurt; my throat ached with the effort not to cry. I wished she wouldn't be so nice. Ben and Archie and the other kids were coming down and I wanted to get out of there before I had to face them too.

'Thanks again, Cheryl. I'll be in touch, OK?'

I pulled the front door open and rushed out into the early morning sunshine. Squinting against the brightness, which glared like a spotlight into my eyes, I dashed down the path, holding my carrier bag of things. I hadn't taken everything that Cheryl had bought for me, only the necessities.

It was stupid of me to go without a proper plan but the dragging sense that I was a burden on these kind people's lives had become worse than the prospect of finding a new place to stay. I only knew that I needed to find my sister and I walked quickly down the pavement out of the estate and on to the nearby main road. From here I could get a bus back to my own village. I'd wondered if Hephzi was staying away simply because she couldn't find me. I'd been haunted by the thought that she'd somehow been left behind, trapped in our room in the vicarage, pawing at the window to be let out. If I wanted to see her then I would have to walk back there. That was the only direction I knew and I started the trek though the sun felt warm on my shoulders and head; it would be hot later. The fields to either side of me were full of oilseed rape and my eyes began to stream and my nose to run; the pollen was a tormenting tickle at the back of my throat. The bright yellow fields reflected the growing glare of the day and I squinted as I walked, my eyes fixed on the pavement before me. For a moment I wondered what would happen if The Father drove past, spotted me and stopped. He could easily bundle me into the back of his car and return me to his lair. The thought pulled me up short and I almost turned around and ran back to the safety of Danny's house. This was sheer madness. But something called me forward again and I knew it was Hephzi. I had to go back for her.

The heat began to hurt but I kept on and eventually the sign welcoming visitors to our village appeared. Thirsty, I licked my dry lips, trying not to think about water. Then an idea came to me, all at once, like a sudden downpour of rain and I moved again, faster now that I was almost there. Craig's estate was closer to the outskirts of the village than the vicarage, which lay right at the other end. It made sense to start there; if Hephzi wasn't in the vicarage then that was where she was sure to be.

The streets were quiet, a few mums with buggies strolled past on their way to the park to feed the ducks and to push their children high on the swings. A little girl on a scooter, her plaits flying, whizzed by me as her mother hurried behind. I watched the teenagers as they circled the park on their bikes and the little groups of kids, enjoying the final lazy days of summer as they meandered together towards the village open-air pool, their towels tucked under their arms, bottles of Coke swinging from their fingers. Hephzi and I had never been allowed to go, of course. I trudged on. No one noticed me.

Craig's place was easy to find, Hephzi had taken me there often enough over the past few months. I'd told her to stop making me act like a stalker but she hadn't cared and told me not to be so selfish. I'd given in, like always. Now I stood in front of the front door, doing nothing, waiting for her to pop up and give me some instructions, like a director charming the best performance out of a difficult star. I sniffed. Nothing but the faint haze of roses from the pot by the front door hung in the air. No Hephzi. It was useless. I turned and walked back down the little concrete path between the small squares of green lawn. Craig's bike sat on the road in front of the house and I paused again. It was stupid to come here and not even to check inside, she could be hiding, cross with me for leaving her, that would be the kind of trick she'd play.

Before I could change my mind I turned and scuttled back to the door, pressed the bell hard and waited, listening to the sound of my breathing. No one answered. They could be round the back. I didn't want to open the gate and stroll round the side of the house like I'd been going there all my life, nor did I want to ring the bell again but I made myself do it, holding the little brass button down longer this time and listening to the buzz reverberate inside the house. Somewhere upstairs there was movement; I sensed thuds and heard a door bang, the tumble of footsteps on the stairs, then there was Craig at the door in boxer shorts, barely awake, peering out through the crack between door and wall, not quite seeing me through the fug of sleep.

'Yeah?'

I coughed, my throat still tickled with pollen, and rubbed the back of my hand over my nose. I waited for him to notice me. He pushed his hand through his hair, which flopped into his eyes, I'd never seen him without his stupid hat on and he had nice hair, I supposed, for him. He opened his eyes a little wider and realized it was me.

'What do you want?' His voice was suddenly angry and loud. I stepped back a pace, surprised at the force of it. It took me all my courage to speak.

'Can I come in?'

'Why?'

This was a difficult one. I would have to lie.

'I want to talk to you.'

I waited as he thought about it. I could hear the traffic from far-away roads, the buzzing of bees as they moved in and out of flowers, a baby crying somewhere down the street. I waited without looking at him, staring at the white plastic doorframe and the concrete step. Finally he opened the door and I followed him into the living room. He didn't seem to care that he was in his pants, he just stood there like that was totally normal. I kept my eyes fixed on the window behind him and tried to feel if Hephzi was hiding somewhere.

'Yeah? What is it, then? I thought they'd put you away, that's what they've been saying.'

'Who?'

He didn't give me the satisfaction of an answer and I tried to imagine the village gossip machine at work, Mrs Sparks flicking a switch, firing up the engine and then sending out batches of information, true or false (who cared?), through letter boxes and windows, over garden fences, in the post office and corner shop. They would have buzzed with the story of the crazy vicar's daughter rampaging through the village in her night clothes, kicking up a fuss, being taken off to a secure unit and held there for her own good. Or maybe The Father had pontificated from his pulpit about the perils of the devil and his own daughter marked with his sign, who was at last blessedly incarcerated. Now his congregation would be able to sleep easy in their beds, knowing that the beast within had been caged. I heard the words fall from his barbed-wire jaw, that snare that had held me tight and twisted all my life, as if he were there behind me, snarling in my ear. Craig broke his spell.

'What d'you want, then? Are you just going to stand there all day or what?'

'Water, can I have some water?'

He looked liked I'd just requested the crown jewels or a million quid and while he disappeared into the kitchen I sent out messages to Hephzi, I shouted at her to come out, come out, wherever she was hiding. Nothing. He handed me the water and I drank it in one long gulp while he watched.

'You hungry?'

I nodded. I'd left without breakfast.

This time I followed him into the kitchen and watched him find cereal, bowls, milk. We sat at the table together and ate. He slurped and munched noisily, enjoying his food, helping himself to more as if I wasn't there.

When he'd finished he remembered me again and stared as I spooned up the remaining flakes from the bottom of the bowl.

'You don't look anything like her, you know.'

I laughed. Did he think I'd never noticed? He blushed and tried to defend himself.

'Well, you're twins and that. You should look a bit alike.'

'Not necessarily. We're non-identical.' My voice dripped irony and he grinned and flashed me a little of his reputed charm. I stiffened, not prepared to be won over. If it hadn't been for him Hephzi would still be alive. Before I could censor them, my mouth blurted out those thoughts – words I'd never thought to utter, and immediately he was red, burning like fire, and a tempest of sparks came flashing in my direction.

'What're you saying that for? That's lies, complete bullshit! I didn't do anything, nothing. I loved her. I love her.'

Angry too, I shouted back, 'You got her pregnant, you stupid pig. You put your baby inside her and she didn't realize! She wasn't like other girls, she was innocent and you took advantage of that. You destroyed her.'

'No. That's crap, that's rubbish. Shut up!'

We were both standing and he grabbed my shoulders and started to shake me, his rage pulsing in waves of panic. He wasn't as strong as The Father, his fingers didn't bite into my flesh planting seeds of death, and I wasn't afraid. I shoved back at him and he let go.

'Please, tell me you're lying. Tell me that's not true.'

'It is true. I didn't come to tell you that though, actually, and I'm sorry I did. I'm going now.' I didn't want to watch him crying, I didn't need to see his pain spilling on to the kitchen floor and be obliged to mop it up. I was through with that.

He pulled me back. He was desperate now to keep me there to find out what he thought I knew.

'Tell me it all. Please, I want to know how she died. You should tell me, she loved me.'

I shrugged. 'I bet you've got another girlfriend now. You didn't love her, you just used her. You should have known better.'

He shook his head madly. 'You've got it wrong, got us wrong. She must have told you, she must have said.'

'If your stupid mother hadn't come to the church and hadn't gone interfering like that, she might be OK. She might have stayed alive and had your baby. I suppose it would probably be born by now.'

He winced and I could see that he was afraid of what I was saying. I'd found out all about babies on Archie's computer in his room, all the facts and details and information, and I threw it like bullets in his direction. It was my turn to do the hurting and I was shelling him, my exposed target, and he was paralysed by the force of my fire.

'Why didn't she tell me?'

'She didn't know! I told you, she wasn't like the others.'

'I would have taken care of her and the baby. I'd have done anything.'

'Too late. You screwed up. You should have stayed away from my sister. She was too good for you.'

'I know. I know. I'm sorry.'

Blubbering like a child he crumpled to the floor, his back against the kitchen units, sprawling in a puddle of his own misery. It was what he deserved. I exhaled and with that breath blew out over half a year's worth of pain. I saw it leave me, floating on the air, particles of darkness escaping my body. Lighter and brighter, I turned to go again.

'You shouldn't be such a bitch. Your sister never said you were a bitch.'

I stopped then. Hephzi had spoken to him about me. That meant he had things I wanted, he had words that were, by rights, mine. I levelled my gaze in his direction, the tears were still cascading down his cheeks. I supposed his sadness ought to have moved me.

'She was my sister. She loved me best.'

'She loved me too.'

He was right. She had loved him. But only because she hadn't known better and because she'd had no choice.

'You should have helped her, then, you should have been worthy of her. You weren't though, were you? You destroyed her chances. She thought she could trust you, Craig, but you weren't up for it, you're just a little kid.'

Finally standing he looked at me and held my eye. I let him have my face, all of it, I was sick of hiding. Eventually he stopped snivelling and nodded.

'All right, then. If you're right, let me help you.'

'What?'

'You say it's all my fault and that I should have done something, saved her, changed the way it turned out. I dunno if I could have done that, if there was something more –' his eyes glazed and for a moment he looked lost – 'but since she's gone, I'm going to do the next best. I'm going to help you.'

'No, you're not.'

'But you need help, don't you?'

How did he know? I was sick of being so transparent. 'I'm fine.'

'No, you're not. Or you wouldn't be here. You hate me. You must have been desperate to come.'

Hephzi had always said that he was clever and now I understood. He wasn't just the idiot in the hat with the cigarette and the bad attitude. Annoyed, I scowled and meant to leave but I still needed to know what she'd been saying about me.

'What else did she tell you?'

'Not much. She was private. I asked but I didn't often get an answer. I wanted her to let me meet you properly, you and your family. She said no way.'

Of course she did. 'But she said some things?'

'Yeah, now and then the odd thing would slip. She told me you covered for her.'

I nodded and scowled some more. He nodded back. 'Thanks.'

'I shouldn't have. I should never have let her do it.'

'How could you stop her?'

He was right again.

'Look, you may as well tell me everything. I reckon I've guessed a lot but there are still gaps. I want to know exactly what happened.'

No way. Craig wasn't getting our story, it had been bad enough telling Danny and Cheryl, bad enough having them badgering me about the police and Social Services. I'd been convinced they were going to land me in it, holding back had just about killed Danny. When I didn't speak he asked again.

'Why won't you tell me? Why are you and her so secretive? Now you're here in front of me I can tell you're twins, you have the same faraway look in your eyes, the same way of moving your heads when someone puts you on the spot.' I sneezed and he laughed bitterly. 'You even sneeze the same.'

I wished he'd shut up. The way he spoke made me want to pull up a chair, to sit down and have him tell me stories about my sister. I wanted him to tell me about the life she'd had with him, the secret world she'd kept behind lock and key, an enchanted garden of good times and laughter and hope. We both had exactly what the other wanted but I didn't know if I dared trade. I eyed him again.

'If I tell you what you want to know, then you have to answer my questions too, all of them. Right?'

He paused and thought, studying me intently. I didn't understand why he didn't flinch and turn away, why he didn't seem bothered at the sight of me. That would be something else I could ask. Eventually he spoke.

'OK. Deal. You spill your beans, I'll spill mine.'

'All right. But there's one other thing.'

'Yeah? What?'

'Nothing I tell you goes further than this room. You

have to promise you won't do anything with the things I tell you and that you'll keep it all secret.'

'No.' He shook his head rapidly. 'No way. I'm sick of secrets and sneaking around. I've had it with that. I've turned over a new leaf.'

'What do you mean?'

'I'm starting college properly in a couple of weeks, the one in town. I'm doing the rest of my exams in a year, catching up on all the shit I've missed. Then I'm going to uni. I'm going to work to pay my way too, and I'm going to make it. Life's too short not to try your damnedest to make a go of it. Hephzi knew that.'

'She might have known. But she couldn't do it, could she?' I spat.

'No, but it's what I got from her, to give it a go and keep hoping for the best and to fight for what you want. So that's my plan and I'm sticking to it.'

'Good for you.' I don't know why I sounded so resentful. Maybe I wanted him to be Bad Craig forever, maybe I was angry that it had taken my sister dying for him to grow up.

'Yeah, I know it's all a bit late now, I know that, Rebecca, but I've got to try or I'll go mental. After she died I thought I was, you know, losing it. It was tough. But my mum helped pull me round and I owe her too. Since my dad left she's been the one who's always been there, rooting for me, trusting me. I owe her big time.'

'Did your mum like Hephzi?'

'Of course she did! Who didn't? Hephzi was . . . well, she was glorious, wasn't she, gloriously sweet and funny and smart.'

I jolted at his words. I hadn't expected him to use language like that or to understand the essence of my sister so well.

He continued, carried away now, 'She thought Hephzi was perfect for me, she thought she'd straighten me out. Maybe she did in the end. But I suppose I was a bad influence for a while. I regret that now, we shouldn't have bunked off like we did, I shouldn't have done that.'

'No, you shouldn't. Why couldn't you have just been like a normal boyfriend?'

'What's one of those, then?'

How would I know? I shrugged and he half smiled. 'You're right though, I should have done better, she deserved better.'

'Tell me what you two did together.'

'OK.' He moved to the back door and walked out into the small, square garden. I followed him and he threw himself down on a shady patch of grass. Then he started to talk and didn't stop. All day we sat and he spoke about my sister and I drank up the words, caught the honey that dripped from his lips and held it to my mouth, savouring the sweet warmth that soothed my burning heart. He took me with them, joyriding through the countryside to seaside towns and city lights. He made me see the world from over his shoulder, as Hephzi had when she'd held tight round his waist as they sped on his bike, her eyes a-glitter with the stars of their future. When he'd led me through every moment, shown me her secrets, held her heartbreak out for me to see, given me her joy and her laughter, I sat back in the afternoon sun in his garden where they'd first kissed. I felt the grass under my fingers and hoped she'd heard him, hoped she could see what she'd meant.

'Thank you,' I murmured, pulling a daisy and shedding its petals. 'I'm sorry I was so mean. I'm sorry I didn't help more. She never said all this. You were her secret. You were sacred, precious. She meant it when she said she loved you.'

'I hope so. Man, I'm shattered. This has been some day. D'you want a drink?'

He loped inside and returned with two bottles of cold beer. I let the liquid fizz in my mouth and savoured the coldness. He raised an eyebrow.

'Hephz didn't drink, it made her sick.'

'Oh.' I put the bottle down on the grass beside me and shivered slightly as the sun dipped behind the tall trees on the horizon. What were the other things I would never know about my sister? Craig had given me all he had, but there would always be so much left unsaid. It made me sad. Craig touched my arm and pulled me to my feet, leading me inside by the hand. He was kind, kind and good, and I had been wrong.

He went out and bought fish and chips. We ate ravenously in silence and he cleared our plates, finishing what I hadn't managed. The intimacy of that made me blush and I told myself to stop being silly, not to let myself be fooled. He would never like me as he'd liked her, I'd never take her place, and I didn't want to, that wouldn't be right. But sitting with him, eating together, comfortable with one another, made me too happy not to notice. Maybe it was just the thought that I'd found a friend, another one.

'When's your mum back?' I asked.

'She's not, she's away on a course.'

'Oh.'

'You can stay the night if you like.' He saw my face and hurried to clarify, 'In the spare room. It's all right, you can trust me.'

I laughed at the notion that someone like him would ever want to be with someone like me.

'What're you laughing at?' He sounded irritated.

'Just you, protesting too much. I hardly think you're going to rape me, do I? I guess I'm not your type.'

'That's not actually funny, you know. You shouldn't make jokes like that.'

The smile was wiped off my face. 'You're right. I'm sick.' I paused and then let myself say, 'I'm weird, we all know that. But don't blame me – it's being locked up most of my life that's done it.'

He stared at me and we felt the weight of those words between us. It was out there now.

Craig hesitated, unsure, before he asked, 'What do you mean, locked up?'

I drew a deep breath. I would have to explain every-thing all over again. Scratch at the itch that wouldn't go away. That's why I'd come after all, wasn't it? To find Craig and to find the sister I'd lost to him, and now I had to trade. My secrets for his.

'Isn't it obvious? Me and Hephzi didn't have lives until last September. How we ever got to start at that college still bewilders me. Let's just say that The, I mean, our parents didn't think we needed the outside world.'

'I knew they were over-protective.' He sounded cautious, feeling the way forward into this new territory.

'That's the understatement of the century. If my father and mother had had their way we'd never have left the vicarage.'

'I get it. What else?'

'Oh. Are you sure you're ready for this?'

'Totally.'

I told him my story then and he listened with as much attention as I had before, the only movements to betray his tension were his leg and his beating foot enacting a rapid tarantella, halting and stalling, then twitching and tapping on the floor. I let him have the lot. The years and years of words and fists, the strap, the silence, the fear, the punish-ments and crimes, and then, finally, the last hard hours of Hephzi's life. He lost it then, totally lost it, and when he flew out of the room I was too slow to stop him and too stupid to remember that he hadn't promised not to tell. I ran after him down the path outside his house and threw myself on to his bike behind him. He didn't stop and push me off, just revved the engine so loud and strong that I nearly toppled, feeling the throb of the machine through my body, and had to grab him as tight as I would my life if someone were trying to take it from me, as tight as I should have held Hephzi.

It was obvious where we were heading and when I stumbled off the bike outside the vicarage I felt no surprise, just an awful numbness that spread from my scalp to my feet in preparation for what I hoped would be the last battle.

Craig stared at me, his eyes brilliant and feverish in the late summer darkness.

'The tree?' he asked.

'No.' I let him follow me to the front door. It was locked and I leant on the old bell, which stood proud of the brickwork of the porch. It clanged loud enough, but no one emerged to let us in. In fact the whole place was in darkness, closed and tired, asleep for the night. There was no fear pulling at my arm, trying to drag me to safety and silence and, liberated, I walked rapidly round the side of the house to the back. Craig followed, still moving raggedly; he was smarting with anger and the need to inflict pain. I stopped and held his arm.

'Let me do this, OK? It's not worth you ruining your life for.'

'I want to kill them,' he growled through his clenched teeth. I nodded, understanding.

'You can't. If you do you'll end up in prison and you'll end up being the one who suffers most. You mustn't waste hate on them, and you mustn't touch either of them. Promise me?'

He shook his head and looked as if he might break open there in the church gardens like a half healed wound. His pain was ravenous and raw.

'Think about your future, the one you told me about. Don't throw it away. Craig, please.'

Eventually he seemed just calm enough to continue and I moved forward again towards the back of the house. The musk of the wild roses that grew in the garden flooded my senses and I tried not to think of Hephzi and me leaning from our window, two little girls too hot to sleep, eager for the summer and reaching for the air. It was this air we'd smelled together and I gathered large breaths of it in the hope of saving some little morsel for later, something that might linger in the folds of memory to sweeten my sadness.

The back door was locked too, and Craig pounded on it, swearing madly as I shushed him and tried to decide what our next move should be. I was surprised no one had emerged and come to investigate the hullabaloo; it wasn't that late, after all, The Parents wouldn't usually be in bed by now. He would probably be drinking and she would be chasing some pointless task in an attempt to wipe away the indelible stains of their existence. Craig tried the door again and eventually it gave, the old wood falling inwards like an old man finally accepting defeat.

Inside the air was cold and dank and I smelled the musty stench of my childhood. The smell pierced the wall of control I'd carefully constructed and I threw my hands to my face.

'It's OK, Reb, it's OK.' For a moment I thought it was Hephzi speaking, she was the only one who'd called me that, the childhood name for me that she'd used since we could talk. But it was Craig who grabbed my hand and held it tight and led me through the kitchen, hunting for whatever we'd come to find.

We both jumped when she emerged from out of the shadows wrapped in the same old dressing-gown, tied tight round her scrawny frame.

'Who's there?' she hissed into the darkness of the echoing hallway. 'What do you want? Get out before I call the police.'

I was shocked that she still looked the same, but after all it had been a couple of months since we had last seen one another. She was thin and blue and papery pale. The fact that she didn't recognize me straight away was a small triumph; my face was the same, of course, but my strength was all new. I wasn't going to let The Mother make me hate myself any more. I drew myself up taller still.

'It's me.' My voice was clear and echoed in the space. I could hear myself properly at last and her retort was weak in comparison. *Good*, I thought.

'What do you want?' she repeated. 'Get out. Get out of here now.'

'Where is he?' I wasn't hiding any more, gone were the days of ducking into shadows, and I wanted her to know it.

'Not here. If he were here he'd kill you. Now scram.'

Stepping towards her I still felt no fear.

'What have you come here for?' she rasped. 'Just leave me be. You've burned your bridges here, get out and leave me alone.'

'No. Why should I?' Hephzi would be locked up or hiding somewhere in the vicarage, I was sure. I pushed past her and started to climb the stairs, my feet naturally finding the spots that made no sound. Craig pounded behind me, unafraid of the trouble the creaks and moans of the house might uncover. The Mother followed behind us both, griping and grim. Our bedroom door was shut tight and I pushed the handle; I was convinced that Hephzi would be inside. She wasn't at Craig's so this was where she must still be.

But there was nothing. Whitewashed walls silently regarded me, blank and eerie in the half light. Craig flipped the switch and the naked bulb sputtered into life only to reveal more of the same. They'd made it like we'd never lived. Running my hands over the walls I searched frantically for signs of Hephzi and her baby but no bump or bulge betrayed their hiding places. And where was my child, the one I'd never held or known, the one which The Mother had buried somewhere on a black dark night? I'd watched her take a spade and scrabble in the dirt, then throw the bundle into the shallow grave, covering her tracks like a cat piling its litter. She hadn't buried the evidence deep enough though and my baby had returned to haunt me in the whispering walls. By the window I stopped and stared out, as if the tree might tell me its secrets. The branches nodded slowly and shook their green arms, tapping at the window with empty fingers. I understood.

Of course they weren't here. Of course. I had grown beyond this room and I had grown free, more free and alive than I'd ever believed might be possible. This room did not hold my sister or our children, their ghosts had flown. Now that I knew they were safe, I saw that the nightmares could end.

Craig came behind me and rested his hand on my arm.

'Come on, let's go. He's not here. I'll come back.'

'Wait a second,' I said and dropped to my knees, pulling at the floorboards in the corner of the room. I wouldn't go without her things.

Relief stole my breath when my fingers closed around Hephzi's chain and I quickly palmed it. Then I stood and stared at The Mother.

'Before I go I want to know. Why did you hate us? Why did you hate me?'

Her mouth twisted.

'You're black. Black creatures. No one wanted you, either of you, but you came anyway. I had to pay for you every day of my life.'

Her answer told me nothing; she was mad, I thought, completely mad.

'We were little girls. We weren't bad or evil or wrong!' I yelled at her. 'You let Hephzi die!'

She screamed then and came at me with fingers that had twisted into claws and were muscled with hate. Craig pulled her away, threw her to the floor and dragged me free from the room. As he did so the world of my past, our palace, our prison, diminished to a cold white space.

'You're sick!' he shot at my mother as we left. 'I'm warning you now, watch your back, I'm not done with you.'

She spat at him and we hurried down the stairs, needing to escape, needing fresh air.

'If that had been your dad, I'd have killed him.'

'No. No, Craig. That wouldn't achieve anything.'

'How can you be so calm?'

'Because that was my life. I've had a long time to get used to it. It's all there's ever been.'

'Why didn't anyone stop them? How could they just ruin your lives like that? I don't get it.'

His distress on my behalf was further proof that he was one of the good guys. Shyly I touched his sleeve, 'It doesn't matter now, Craig. Please, let it go. All right?'

'I can't.'

I let him nurture his anger and thoughts of revenge. The only thing I cared about now was the loss of my sister. I'd been so sure that she would be there, so sure she'd explode in joy when she saw us together, come to rescue her at last. I was glad she was free but I still wanted to find her, some vestige at least, and to say a better goodbye. I had to tell her how sorry I was that I hadn't saved her, I owed her that. I hadn't been able to tell her so at her funeral, eight months ago, and I hadn't had the guts to say it all the time she'd been with me, helping me and telling me to grab my life before The Father finished things first. Of course I couldn't tell Craig what was going on, he'd have consigned me to the nuthouse along with my crazy mother, but I knew my apology to Hephzi was long overdue.

Going back to Craig's seemed the only plausible option now evening had fallen, but I asked him to wait for me a little longer. Next door at the care home it would be just after bedtime and I knew Danny was working a late shift. Michaela let me in, grinning and hugging and patting my cheeks, saying how good it was to see me, how nice, how happy. I asked for Danny and she pointed to the kitchen. He wheeled round when he heard me say his name.

'Here you are, then! You turned up. Cheryl's been worried sick.'

'I'm so sorry. I just came to tell you I'm OK.'

'All right, love. I'm glad to see you, but you had us going there. Cheryl was all for calling the police.'

'She didn't, did she?'

'No. I calmed her down. I said you wouldn't have gone far, not without money or a place to go. So, what have you been doing?'

'I went back there.' I jerked my head in the direction of the vicarage.

'You what?' His face paled. I knew working so close by

was torture for him and that every day he had to restrain himself from going round there and giving the vicar a taste of his own medicine, that's what Archie had told me anyway. Of course The Parents, instead of doing the decent thing and moving on, had stayed put, brazening out the rumours, telling people I was mad and that Danny was some sort of child molester who had me under his evil spell. Most disregarded the lies, Archie said, but I still felt bad for Danny and the mess I'd brought to his door.

'It's OK. I had some things to pick up. That's all. He wasn't there.'

'Thank God for that. Bloody hell, Rebecca, you're not one for a quiet life, are you? Now why don't you wait in the lounge? I'll be off in half an hour or so, I can give you a lift back.'

'No, Danny. It's OK. Thanks anyway.'

'What d'you mean?'

'I'm staying at a friend's tonight and then tomorrow, well, who knows. I might go to see my aunt.'

'Right.' His happy, open features were clouded by a frown. 'Are you sure you'll be OK?'

'Yes. Thank you for everything you did for me. You've been the best dad I could have had.'

'Stop it!' His cheeks flushed pink and he smiled sadly at me. 'We'll still be around for when you need us, I want you to come whenever you need something, anything, all right? Promise?'

I promised and he wrapped me in one of his bear hugs,

the best hugs in the world. Then he shoved twenty quid into my palm. I tried to thrust it back but he wouldn't hear of it.

'You'll need a bit of ready cash, love, till you get yourself sorted, and that's not much either. But let me know if you need more, I'll help you out. Archie and the kids are going to miss you, you know.'

His kindness was too much and I looked down, trying not to let the tears fall. I was strong now, he'd helped me to get strong and I wanted him to be proud. Before I left I nipped into Cyrilla's room; she was half asleep already. I dropped a kiss on her soft, lined cheek and whispered goodbye. I think she smiled and almost raised a hand in farewell.

Slowly I was ticking things off. Slowly I was getting myself ready. I did mean it, I was leaving. I was stepping out of the shadows and I was finding a life. The one that had been waiting for me all this time.

The next morning Craig slept late but I was up with the sun. I knew where I was going now. The walk wasn't too long and it wasn't too hot yet. My scalp and arms and face were sore from yesterday's sunshine but the throb and itch simply reminded me that I was still alive. Craig had given me some cream to rub in and that had soothed my skin as I'd slept. I felt almost good.

Before I left forever there were still some things I needed to do. The village had grown too small for me, the memories too large, and I wanted something else now. I might find a doctor or go back to college and study something I was interested in. Craig's plans had inspired my own; if he could go to uni then so could I. Craig didn't look at me like I was a monster and nor had Archie; I'd been wondering if maybe one day I'd find someone who might love me in spite of my face. Life could begin all over again if you were lucky enough, and I had decided to be lucky. But before any of that future could happen I had to make one last effort to find Hephzi.

A simple headstone marked Hephzibah's grave and the grass had grown new and wild over the fresh soil. I read just her name and our birthday and then the day she'd died. There were no special words. I unclasped her silver chain from round my neck and crouched in the dewy grass. The wet fronds tickled my calves as I made a hole in the damp soil with my fingers; a light summer rain had fallen overnight and the air smelled as if someone had scrubbed it clean. With dirt under my nails, I held her necklace to my lips, kissed it and whispered a message before burying it as deep as it would go.

'Hephz, are you there?' I whispered into the earth. There was no response. I stretched myself out on the ground beside her, and called again.

'Hephzibah, it's Rebecca. I'm here to say goodbye. Please talk to me, don't be angry that I'm leaving, will you?'

Still she was quiet.

'I've come to tell you I'm sorry. I know I should have saved you. If I'd been braver. If I'd called for the ambulance sooner. I'm sorry. I love you, Hephz.'

The birds called and sang in the trees, and the wind pulled my hair gently. I waited a little longer, every cell alive with anticipation.

Hephzi was there. Of course she was. She'd been there all the time. In the wind on my skin and the sun in my face, in the quick shot of stars I'd seen from my hospital bed, in the dark of my shadow and the stretch of my stride as I'd run from the vicarage, finally breaking free. As I lay in the sun beside her I felt the wings of her beauty lift me and, as I felt them beat with hope, I knew I could go on. Hephzibah was elsewhere, but also in me.

Craig was up when I got back to his house and he made us breakfast together again. He was quiet and I knew he was brooding over everything I'd told him. I was sorry he'd had to hear all those awful things about Hephzi's life and I told him so.

'It's OK. I wanted to know.' He looked up at me and I saw the fire in his eyes and realized he still wanted revenge. But I'd seen enough blood to last me forever and there was no way I was going to spill any more. He was right in a way though; there were still some things left undone.

I thought of Auntie Melissa. She'd promised she'd help. I didn't need her to save me now, but I did want her story. I asked Craig if I could use the phone and swallowed my pride and bitter dislike.

She was startled to hear from me, that much was obvious, and for a second I wondered if her profession of interest had all been a sham.

'Are you OK, Rebecca?'

'Yes. Thank you.'

'How can I help? Are you still living with your friends?'

'No, I left.'

'Oh.'

'It's OK, it's just their place was small, I'd been there a few months.'

'I see. So where are you now?'

'At Hephzi's boyfriend's. I can't stay long though.'

Neither of us spoke for a while and I tried to imagine what she was doing. Was she pulling panicked faces at Uncle Simon, or screwing her forehead up in worry? Did she want me or not?

'Shall I come and see you? See if I can help?' she finally offered.

'OK, if you like.'

'All right. Give me the address. It won't be until tomorrow though. Is that all right?'

'Yes. I can stay another night here.'

As I put the phone down I thought of Granny. I could have run straight to her, she'd have taken me in without a second thought. I could have cared for her in her old age, gone to college during the day or studied at home and sat with her in the evenings doing a crossword or watching the telly. It wasn't fair.

'So she's coming, then?' Craig asked and I nodded and left the room.

Of course I couldn't sleep that night. Nightmares no longer kept me awake but instead I fretted over Auntie Melissa. I knew what I wanted and that was answers. But I also needed a home and a life and she could give me neither.

I watched TV all morning, still alive, still waiting.

At ten o'clock the doorbell sounded. They were both there, Melissa and Simon. Craig wasn't up and I opened the door with my jacket ready. The sun wasn't so hot today, grey banks of cloud were assembling themselves in the distance, an army establishing its lines of defence. The air was heavy and damp; it smelled like rain.

We walked down the driveway to the car. Simon drove, Melissa twisted in her seat to look at me. Her smile could break as easily as a heart.

'You OK?'

I nodded.

'Where should we go?'

'Away from here.'

Simon nodded and drove steadily out of the village, in the opposite direction to the vicarage. Once we were in town he pulled over and we all got out. I had no idea where we were and I let them lead the way out of the car park and into a cafe. This wasn't a good place, we should have stayed at Craig's. Simon went up to the counter and ordered drinks and breakfast. Melissa and I sat facing one another.

'Thanks for coming,' I said in the end, because I knew she wanted to cry.

'I'm sorry it took me so long.'

I tried a small smile.

'I'm here now though. We're here. We'll help any way we can.'

'OK.'

'What do you need?'

'You have to tell me everything.'

'What do you mean?'

'On the phone, you said things. You said she never should have married him. What did you mean?'

Melissa hadn't been expecting that. She looked down, then over to Simon at the counter, then back at her hands and twisted her wedding ring.

'Oh, it's old news now, it's not important.'

'Just tell me,' I insisted.

'I don't want to upset you, Rebecca.'

'You won't. I can take it, whatever it is.' I understood that Melissa still had no idea of what my life had been. If she thought her words could ever cut me, she was wrong.

'All right. If that's what you want.'

'It is.'

So then came the story of Roderick Kinsman and Maria Detherby. My mother had been eighteen when she'd got involved with the church group. Melissa remembered Roderick coming round to the house and collecting her sister before the services, then walking her home afterwards. Even though he was good looking he was stiff, she said, stiff and unsmiling, always wearing a long heavy coat and a shirt and tie.

'And those eyes –' she shuddered – 'when he looked at me the hair on the back of my neck used to stand up. I always thought there was something really creepy about those eyes.'

I knew what she meant.

Melissa told me that Roderick refused to come in for

tea or hot chocolate and refused to come for Sunday lunch. It was obvious he disapproved of Granny and of Melissa too. Melissa wore make-up and liked the Stone Roses; Maria wore a crucifix and hid her sister's CDs.

'Why was she like that?'

'I don't know. It might have been because Dad died – our dad, your granddad. She'd been his favourite, he adored her. When he had his stroke it affected us all, but Maria, she took it really badly. She just became obsessed with religion and those meetings. I wouldn't have minded if it hadn't been so obvious they were being played for fools. She got money off Mum to give to this guy, their pastor. They had funny ideas, fasting for days at a time and all that laying-on-hands stuff. She reckoned she could speak in tongues. Can you imagine! She wouldn't see her old friends or go to her old activities. We tried to get her to do other things but she just wasn't interested.'

'So what happened next, then?'

'Well. Your mother's always had a bit of an impetuous streak. Maybe like Hephzi.'

She smiled but I did not smile back. The Mother and Hephzi were nothing alike. I stopped myself from asking what the hell she knew about my sister but Melissa realized her mistake.

'Sorry, no, I don't mean that, really. But she was strong-willed and stubborn. When Roderick proposed she said yes straight away; even though your gran told her to go to university first and find herself a good career she wouldn't hear of it. Roderick was still studying too, only just in the third year of his course at university.'

She leant towards me, as if she were telling me something important. 'Your mother isn't stupid, you know, Rebecca, she did well at school, she could have made a decent living without him.'

'So you couldn't stop her?'

'No. But we went to the wedding, even though the night before she and your gran had an awful row. She warned her about Roderick, she'd sensed it somehow.'

'He hated Granny.'

'I know.'

'It's his fault she died.' I couldn't stop myself from saying it, although I knew that Melissa wouldn't understand.

'What d'you mean? Mum fell down the stairs, you know; she had a heart attack and no one found her in time to help. She never would wear one of those emergency tags, the silly old thing.'

'If it hadn't been for him she'd have still been alive, I know it.'

'Maybe. That doesn't matter, it's past now.'

Melissa understood nothing. She was stupid and dull, I thought, and I regretted starting this conversation; it would be hours before I found out anything important at the rate she told a story. Sensing my frustration she started up again. Simon joined us with the drinks. I sipped my tea and listened.

'It was after they were married that she found out she

was pregnant. She came running back to us, weeping and wailing. Of course they'd not slept together before the wedding – God forbid that Roderick's wife might not be a virgin! But, like I said, Maria was a bit naughty. She did what she liked despite the religion, or maybe because of it, and she told us that Roderick was not the father, couldn't possibly be because she was three months gone. She was so slim she was barely starting to show but she knew she'd have to tell him soon.'

More secret babies, I thought, *but this time it's me and Hephz*.

If Melissa had expected her story to shock or to hurt, it did neither. I found myself merely curious.

'Who was the father, then?'

'Your father was Roderick and Maria's pastor, the leader of the funny church group they'd got themselves involved with. Roderick hit the roof when he realized that Maria had been sleeping with him behind his back. He was still studying for his degree and they were living like paupers in his student digs. He wouldn't take a penny from your gran, even when he found out Maria was expecting. Your gran was desperate to help, she worried all the time what would become of them. He was training to be in the Church, well, you know that, of course, and I've no idea why he was mixed up with that other funny bunch in the first place. I've nothing against the Church. Me and Simon were married in one, after all!'

I looked at her. She'd said that as if I should remember. I shrugged.

'We did invite you. You were only tiny tots, but I asked for you to be bridesmaids. I thought it would be sweet.'

Hephzi would have loved that. I shook the picture of her in a pink satin dress holding a posy of flowers out of my mind.

'Why didn't he abandon her? Abandon us? It would have been better for everyone.' I was frustrated at the thought of another life, surely one less thwarted for Roderick oKinsman's absence. I thrust the idea of it away. *Get real*, I told myself.

'You're probably right but that's not Roderick, is it? He likes to play the burning martyr, and the pastor came on heavy, I think, he talked about scandal and what a disgrace it would be for all involved. I think he intimated that he could ruin Roderick's chances in the Church full stop. On top of that this bloke, your real dad, was already married and it would have destroyed his career. Roderick understood that. He was terribly angry but your mother thought he'd get over it as time went on.'

That was it, of course. Appearances had to be maintained at all costs, the mask could never slip. And The Father had loved owning the opportunity to punish The Mother for the rest of her days, and us too. All my life I'd been paying with my body and my spirit for her sordid little affair.

'But then you were born . . .' Melissa didn't finish her sentence but I heard what she couldn't bring herself to say. When I was born he couldn't bear it; bringing up another man's children was bad enough, but one that looked like me, well, that was just insult on top of injury.

'So that's the story, then. That's all it is?'

'Yes, that's all.'

It wasn't quite. She hadn't explained why she'd left us there when she could have tried to help. Granny had tried, but where had Auntie Melissa been? Simon shifted awkwardly in his seat. The silence held its questions. I stared from one to another.

'Didn't you care? Didn't you mind that we were there with them? Didn't you see what was going on?'

My voice was small with sorrow. Melissa pushed her chair back, it squealed on the cafe floor, and she ran to the toilets, hiding her face.

I held Simon's gaze.

'She cares, Rebecca. She does. Especially because we won't have kids of our own now. I told her there's only a tiny chance that we'd have a baby with, you know, well . . .'

He nodded towards me as if to illustrate his point, then looked away, behind him, over to the loos, where Melissa had gone. 'Anyway, I said we could get tested – you can get these genetic tests now, you know, and I've told her that I don't mind paying, if it puts her mind at rest, but she won't even talk about it. Because we knew about you, she, well, we, decided it was for the best that we didn't risk it.'

My head throbbed with this new information. I wondered if he realized that he was calmly telling me that it would have been better if I'd never been born. A handy test could have screened me out long ago and then there'd have been one less problem for people to ignore.

'We want to adopt,' he continued, oblivious, 'but it's a wait. It's taking its toll on Mel, she's pretty fragile right now.'

It was time to leave. I stood up and left the cafe and walked out into the town. Rain was still threatening and goose pimples prickled on my arms. People hurried through the market square, not lingering at the stalls today. I stared around me, feeling lost and wondering where the bus station was. Melissa and Simon caught up with me quickly.

'What are you going to do now?' Simon asked.

'I don't know. I need to find a place to live.'

'You can come back with us, if you like?' Melissa's offering pressed towards me and I remembered The Father presenting his fist like a favour too. I needed no such help.

'No thanks. I'll stay round here somewhere, but not back in the village.' My voice was an icy blast in the humid, leaden air and she threw a worried look at her husband.

'Do you have any money?'

I shook my head. Mel took my arm and pulled me to a halt beside her.

'Listen, when your granny died I inherited everything.

She didn't trust Roderick with it. I know she'd have wanted me to take care of you with that money.'

I looked at Melissa. Her eyes were Hephzi's chocolate brown.

'Will you take it? Take the money?'

She withdrew as much as she could that afternoon and promised more as soon as I was set up with a bank account. They dropped me back at Craig's, the squeaking smear of the windscreen wipers beating out a rhythm of pain. Simon coughed and turned on the radio. There were no kisses goodbye and I watched their car putter off, smaller than before. I went round the back, my pockets stuffed with cash.

'All right?'

'Yeah, thanks.'

'What'd she say?'

'He isn't our father.' Essentially that was all it amounted to, the rest was just padding.

'Oh.'

'I'm glad.' I pointed out the obvious, just to hear the words aloud.

'Yeah.'

'And she gave me money. It was my gran's, it's not charity.' I'd had enough of charity to last me forever and I would take only one more thing from Melissa, but that could wait a little while longer.

'Good.'

'Will you help me find a flat?'

'Course.'

Before that happened though, I had one final matter to deal with. I'd saved the worst until last. I decided to tell Craig, just in case I didn't return.

'I'm going to go back again. Tomorrow. I'm going to his service in the morning.'

He stared at me and so I repeated myself.

'You can't do that, not on your own.'

'Why not? You can't stop me, Craig, I'm not afraid of him anyway.'

'Well, I'm coming with you.'

'I'm not going on some vigilante mission, you know,' I warned.

'I know. But I'm still coming.'

I felt calm as I walked towards the church the next morning, calmer than before anyway. This time I knew I would leave as and when I pleased and that no one could hold me against my will. The streets were full of Sunday peace and the fingers of fear which had once grasped my belly as I'd trodden this path home from college no longer wrung my insides. I saw Danny and Cheryl outside the church doors, waiting for us. Craig had insisted that they be there too. 'Back-up,' he'd said and, even though I'd shaken my head, I'd let him make the call.

Danny gave me a big hug, Cheryl too, and we stood for a moment outside holding each other. Then I pulled away and dragged open the heavy door.

The service had already started. I could hear his voice intoning the prayers and walked steadily towards it, my feet quiet on the stone floor. A few bodies sat scattered in the pews and I was struck by the smallness of them; his congregation had dwindled further still. It had gradually been depleting for years and his attempts to recruit new supporters had ceased to be effective some time ago. But there had always been more than this. Something must have happened. I spotted my mother's bent back and bowed head; she sat in her usual position on the front bench. Mrs Sparks sat on the other side with her husband and I stood in the aisle for a moment deciding which seat to choose. The others were behind me, waiting to follow my lead. As I moved forward the man at the altar became aware of my presence and the prayer died on his lips as we caught one another's eyes. His were the same penetrating blue they'd always been. I held that gaze firmly and walked forward to take a seat just behind my mother, right where I could see him. I knew people were gawping now but I didn't care; their stares fell off my skin like raindrops running from leaves. Danny, Cheryl and Craig sat behind me and I felt Danny's hand rest for a moment on my shoulder.

This would be the last time I would ever see the man who had masqueraded as my father and I drew a deep sigh and turned my face up towards his.

He was expecting me to cower, he was waiting for that reaction, and I watched his snarl unfurl as his lips began to move again. When I simply offered him my gaze in return, a gaze which only demanded the recognition of my right to exist, his voice faltered once more, and my mother swung her head round to see why. I let her look too, and she turned back quickly as he dropped his book and crouched on the floor to retrieve it. He stood again, rustled through the pages to try to find his place, then coughed and looked up. But his eyes came nowhere near mine. I watched him try to smile.

'Forgive me,' he continued, eventually, 'let us pray.' His words had never been more false.

A few people pulled themselves to their feet. They listened to the passage he read haltingly from the Bible and I felt sorry for the little old ladies and the devoted remnants of his flock as he joined in with their Amen. And then we waited for the sermon.

Whatever words he had prepared, no one ever knew. He stood there frozen in silence, his mouth fallen slack, as everybody stared and I heard them begin to whisper.

Then I stood and walked away, as slowly as I had come.

On Monday, with Craig's help, I found somewhere far enough away for me to feel safe. It was small and clean. I could invite Cheryl and Danny there. Melissa sent the money for the deposit and then Craig helped me to move in. His mum gave me stuff she didn't need and I planned to get the rest whenever. I didn't require much.

My final request of Auntie Melissa was that she send me Granny's photo album. It arrived wrapped in tissue paper with a kind note, repeating again how sorry Melissa was and inviting me to stay with them at Christmas or whenever I liked. I screwed it up and chucked it aside. Craig and I stared at the album together.

'Go on, look inside,' he said.

I turned the pages; they were as thin and easy to crease as I'd remembered. The past sprung up at me, newly made, and I examined the old pictures of Auntie Melissa and The Mother, pretty little babies, frilly in pink, chubby and cute. Granny looked so young, with a perm and lots of pink lipstick, laughing at whoever was taking her picture, with her daughters on her knee. Then I stared at pages I didn't ever remember seeing before. There were more pictures of The Mother and Melissa; I guessed they were about twelve or thirteen, and their arms were wrapped around one another as they stood in swimsuits on a beach, or sat straight and proud on horseback, or posed seriously in school uniform with my gran and the grandad I'd never met. Maria was quite pretty, in a quiet, wispy way, but she had a lovely smile. I didn't recognize that girl as the mother who'd never been able to love me. I glanced at the other pictures, ones of The Parents, stiff in wedding clothes, a few of Melissa at her graduation, and then more of the ones I'd ripped to smithereens when I was small. Granny must have made copies. I slammed the pages shut; I'd look at them later when I was alone.

As I walked Craig to the door, he paused just outside.

'Here.'

'What's that?'

'A good-luck present. Take it.'

I took the book: Shakespeare, *Twelfth Night*. I looked at him, puzzled.

'You'll like it. It has a happy ending. And look.'

He flicked open the book and inside the front cover something lay loose, a shiny piece of paper. I pulled it out and stared at it for a long, light moment. Hephzi's face laughed up at me from the photograph, ecstatic with happiness and hope, her eyes more alive than I'd ever seen them.

'Don't you want this?'

'I have others. I can reprint it anyway. I have loads of her. You can put it in the album.'

'Oh.' I wish he'd said so before.

'I'll send you more. Let me know your email address when you get sorted, OK?'

'All right. Thanks. It's beautiful.'

'I know. She was.' We hugged for a long time then and the next thing I knew he was off. I closed the door softly behind him, locked it tight and attached the safety chain. Holding my picture of Hephzi I knew I wouldn't paste it in Granny's album but that I would find a perfect frame somewhere, and place her where I could see her every day. I knew I would be all right here for now.

I never intended to go back and I suppose I needn't have done so, even after the fire. But I wanted to check, I had to be sure they'd really gone.

It had been a few weeks since my trip to the church when I'd last faced Roderick Kinsman. Autumn had set in but the sun was shining and the air smelled fresh and the occasion could not dull the brightness of the day. It was over nine months since Hephzibah's funeral and here I was, again.

There were few mourners. Just some church officials, and Mrs Sparks, who avoided my eye, and some locals who had come for a good nosy, hungry hens pecking through dirt in search of more seeds for a story which would grow later like weeds. Auntie Melissa and I stood near the back. I could have pitied my mother, but she didn't deserve it and I looked on impassively as the new vicar searched for something to say about her. He found a few clichés: determined community worker, devoted wife, blah blah blah. At least he didn't dare suggest that she'd been a beloved mother.

After the service the other people drifted off like dust and the new vicar approached me. He stumbled through an apology of sorts and I listened and nodded; he was not to blame, after all. Eventually I was left alone with my aunt. Perhaps I didn't speak enough to her then, as far as I could tell there wasn't any point, but I think I managed to be quite polite. She didn't look that bothered about her sister, although I'd spotted her dabbing at her eyes during the service. Keeping up appearances obviously runs in the family.

Some people still chose to believe that the fire was an accident, faulty wiring or something like that. It's funny how the truth can be so evasive – a will-o-the-wisp, receding even as you inch ever closer towards it. Not even the arrest of their vicar was quite enough to alter their reality.

But I was glad that Roderick had survived his own fire. It was strange that the flames hadn't licked him up, as he'd intended, and allowed him to escape what he knew was coming. I was glad he languished in prison awaiting trial, even if it did mean I had to reveal the scars which he'd burned into my heart, the wounds which had finally begun to heal.

'You'll talk now, Rebecca, won't you?' the policewoman had said when she'd come to tell me the news, and I'd nodded my assent. That story was the past, but I accepted that it could still be told while I worked on the future. Hephzi would have wanted me to speak up for her and I'd always been brave enough for both of us.

I didn't let them bury what was left of The Mother with

Hephzi. Instead we burned the scraps that remained after the conflagration and I chucked the urn holding her ashes into the nearest bin I could find. After that there wasn't much more to do. I walked up the road and looked around me, seeing the village with fresh eyes, and whispered my goodbyes to the places as I passed them: the college, the shop, the library I'd always yearned to visit, the chemist where Hephzi had stolen, Mrs Sparks' house. Before I left I returned to the mess that now stood where the vicarage had once loomed. Everything else had been eaten by the flames but the tree, our tree, still stood. A little blackened, a little hurt, but still strong and proud. A gust of wind rustled its leaves and a few spiralled to the ground as it swayed its sorrow at my departure. I think it wished me luck as well.

From across the road a man on his moped waved, then revved his bike and shot away. I would see him again. There would be time for that and for other things too. Just for now I was glad to be on my own.

And so I walked away from the rubble of the past. I saw that the day was bright and the sun was stronger than autumn ought to have allowed. It caught on the stone of the houses in the distance and warmed them gold. Black was a bruise but blue was the sky and, as the future opened its arms, I stepped forward and smiled.

Acknowledgements

Humungous thanks to Amanda Punter, Mari Evans and Alex Clarke at Penguin. Thank you for your passion, expertise, wisdom and insight. Thank you to all the other brilliant Penguin and Puffin staff who have supported and assisted with the publication of *Black Heart Blue*.

To Amanda Preston at Luigi Bonomi Associates. Thank you for loving *Black Heart Blue*, for not giving up on me and for your brilliant agenting skills.

To my super sisters Emily and Margaret Barry. Thanks for always wanting to read what I write and for making me believe other people might want to read it too! Thanks to Gill and Dave for everything – you're the best. To my BFM Juliette Tomlinson, whose opinion and help count for a great deal. To Sarah Mitchell, who has been an avid reader of every draft and believed in the book from the outset – thank you.

To the Gilded Palace of Sin for dark tunes.

To Rita Gabrielle Wilson. If ever there was a woman who loved words, it was you.

Above all my darling husband, Alistair. Thank you for putting up with me, for knowing about genetics, for reading and believing. And thank you to my wonderful daughters, who make me laugh every day.

If you've been affected by any of the issues in this book, or would like to find out more, you may find these links helpful.

Treacher Collins syndrome

- BBC Health: www.bbc.co.uk/health/physical_health/conditions/treachercollins1.shtml
- NHS disfigurement support: www.nhs.uk/Livewell/facialdisfigurement

Support for teens dealing with physical/emotional/sexual abuse and/or bereavement

- Childline: www.childline.org.uk
- Samaritans: www.samaritans.org
- NSPCC: www.nspcc.org.uk
- Al-Anon UK, for family and friends of alcoholics: www.al-anonuk.org.uk
- National Association for the Children of Alcoholics: www.nacoa.org.uk
- Refuge – a domestic-abuse charity: www.refuge.org.uk
- Young people's counselling at Relate: www.relate.org.uk/young-people-counselling/index.html
- Mind – a mental-health charity: www.mind.org.uk/help/diagnoses_and_conditions/sexual_abuse
- Winston's Wish – a charity for bereaved children: www.winstonswish.org.uk

Reading Group Questions

1) What were your first impressions of both Rebecca and Hephzibah? Did your opinion of them change as the novel progressed? Discuss these characters' similarities and differences.

2) Rebecca and Hephzibah have a complex relationship. They are allies and, at times, a thorn in each other's side. What do you think about the way Hephzibah treats her sister? Does Rebecca react to this treatment in the way you would expect her to?

3) Rebecca refers to her parents not as Mum and Dad but as The Mother and The Father. What do you think this form of address adds to the novel?

4) Craig is the boy who wins Hephzibah's heart but who also comes between the two sisters. How important do you think Craig's role in the novel is? Do you think things would have turned out differently if Hephzibah and Rebecca had never met him?

5) The position that Rebecca and Hephzibah's father holds in the village – that of vicar and a pillar of the community – puts him in a position of trust. Did this make a difference to you in terms of how you reacted to his treatment of his daughters, and indeed of his wife and her wider family?

6) The girls' grandmother seems to be the only character in the novel who stands up to Roderick. How much influence do you think she has on Rebecca and Hephzibah in terms of their desire to escape? Do you think her fate helped or hindered the sisters' will to break free?

7) Danny becomes an unlikely friend to Rebecca when she works at the care home. Do you think Danny plays a big part in Rebecca's story?

8) From the beginning of the novel we know how Hephzibah's story ends, but what did you think about the ending to Rebecca's story? Was it the ending you expected?

Don't miss the next
unforgettable novel from

LOUISA REID

coming in **2012**

Lies
LIKE
Love

FOR FICTION TO MAKE YOU

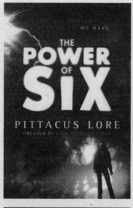

GASP out loud
STAY up late *and*
MISS your stop

Get into **Razorbill**